A Class Action

AASHISH DESAI

A Class Action By Aashish Desai

Published 2021 by Your Book Angel

Copyright © Aashish Desai

Edited by Keidi Keating

Layout by Rochelle Mensidor

ISBN: 979-8-9850627-0-0

This book is dedicated to my father,
Atri Yadvendra Desai (1934-2019),
The greatest man I ever knew.
"If it is to be, it is up to me."

PART I

The Case

Chapter 1

The rental property's unique scent of cardboard and vanilla wasn't something Mack Poyfair had grown used to yet. It also wasn't something he associated with stress and pain. One day, he would come in with his shoulders bowed and they wouldn't straighten up, he knew that. But that day wasn't here yet. This new office was full of hope, and he felt the weight of the morning's divorce proceedings lift. At least that was over now.

"Good morning," he said to the two women. Each sat behind a desk at opposite walls, facing the middle of the common area and each other. His own portion of the office was along the back wall, a bit farther away to afford privacy for clients. As he headed for his desk, Antonia—Poyfair Law Firm's paralegal—cleared her throat and flashed her 1000-watt grin at him. He paused, noticing a man sitting in a chair next to her desk. The man was stout with dark hair, and he held a well-loved Angels cap in his lap.

"This is Isaiah Garza. Mr. Garza would like to speak to you regarding a possible case," Antonia chirped.

Mr. Garza stood, and the two men shook hands. "Hello, Mr. Garza. I'm Mack Poyfair. Let's step over to my desk and have a chat." He gestured for Mr. Garza to walk ahead of him.

"Just call me Isaiah, please," the man said as he made his way to the only unoccupied desk in the office.

Mack made brief eye contact with his associate Gloria. Her expression was not as hopeful as Antonia's. Ever the professional, she nodded and then went back to her computer and files.

Mack sat at his desk and tucked away his briefcase. "Can I get you some coffee or water, Isaiah?" he asked, taking care to use the man's first name as requested.

"No, thank you," Isaiah replied.

Mack smiled. "Down to business then. What can I help you with, Isaiah?"

"I heard about a case you did with some truckers. Against the Ecklehurst Trucking Company?" he said. His voice was low. Mack leaned forward.

"Yes, when I was with Myer and O'Toole," he said.

Isaiah turned the Angels cap in his hands. "I work for a trucking company, and I think they're going to fire me for no good reason," he said.

"Oh?" Mack prompted. It had long been his experience that people as soft-spoken as Isaiah wanted to give their reasons before stating their intentions. Mack's patience was limitless when it came to his clients, or potential clients.

"I came back from my delivery about three weeks ago and left the truck as usual. The next day, the shift manager is saying I damaged the truck when I made the drop off." Isaiah's shoulders squared up and his spine straightened, making him several inches taller. "I did not damage that truck, but they went and wrote me up. Now I've been getting the bad shifts and they've been treating me like shit."

"What do you mean?" Mack prompted. He wasn't even sure what the case was yet, but he would keep Isaiah talking until he knew what the man wanted.

"I mean I'm getting the late shifts, and the worst paying routes. When I bring the truck in and do the DVIR, they question everything on it, getting real picky. 'Was the oil at three-quarters or was it really at five-eighths?' That sort of thing. They're gunning for me and I know they're going to fire me." Isaiah curled the brim of the cap in his tensing hand.

"I see," said Mack.

Isaiah took a deep breath. "I heard you were the guy to call for this sort of thing with truckers."

"What sort of thing is that, exactly?" Mack asked. "What is it you want?"

"I want to file for wrongful termination."

"You have not yet been terminated, correct?" Mack asked.

"Right," Isaiah agreed. "I know it's coming though."

While Mack couldn't file a lawsuit over something that hadn't happened yet, he did know quite a bit about trucking companies after his experience with the Ecklehurst case, and the treatment Isaiah was describing did seem unfair. If he dug hard enough, he might uncover something actionable for Isaiah. "You said you're being given the worst-paying shifts?" he asked.

"Yeah. I have a family to support," Isaiah answered. "If all I ever get are the crap shifts, then I never see my family and I barely make enough to keep us going."

Mack dragged a finger behind his ear and uncapped a pen. "How does that pay work exactly? Are you paid by the load or the hour or...?"

"By the mile."

"Do you have a paystub you could show me?" asked Mack.

"I got my latest one right here." Isaiah pulled an envelope from the breast pocket of his plaid button-down. "Just picked it up before I came here."

"May I?" Mack held out a hand and Isaiah placed the envelope in it. Mack lifted the opened seal and extracted the sheet within. In a single glance, he knew Isaiah had brought him a real case, even if it wasn't the one he thought it was. He set the paystub down on the desk and said, "Here's the deal. We can't go after them for wrongful termination. First of all, you haven't yet been terminated. Second, California is an 'at-will' state, which means they can fire you whenever they want with or without a reason. There are some protected classes, but it's still very difficult for an employee to win that."

Isaiah cast his eyes down and his shoulders followed.

"However," Mack said, "I can see right here that you're not being paid appropriately."

"I'm not?" Isaiah asked, his head rising again.

"Nope, and it looks like something that might extend to your fellow drivers. Tell me about a typical shift for you. What's the first thing that happens when you get to work?" Mack prompted.

"I do the vehicle inspection and get all the reports and the keys I need. Then I check the load."

"About how long would you say that all takes?" asked Mack.

"An hour or more, depending on the load."

Mack rubbed his jaw. "You're not paid for that time."

"That's supposed to be made up by our driving, factored into the mile rate," Isaiah said, pointing to the paper in Mack's hand.

"You're getting paid thirty-two cents a mile," Mack said.

Isaiah nodded.

"This is a case we can win."

Isaiah leaned forward. "How do you know?"

"If your wheels aren't rolling, you're not earning, right?" Isaiah nodded. "When you're doing all this stuff—the inspection, getting the reports, checking the load—are your truck wheels moving?"

"No," Isaiah said.

Mack leaned forward again. "So, you're not making any money then. If the system is set up so you can't earn during that time, that system is illegal. They need to pay you for that time, not just for your driving."

Isaiah's eyes lit up. "So you're going to take my case?"

"I'm taking *a* case and you're going to be involved," Mack said. "With something like this, we're looking at a class-action suit. You're going to be the lead class representative. We're going to have to get others on board, more of the drivers at"—he glanced at the paystub again—"Polson Reed Trucking."

"Class representative?" Isaiah asked.

"Yes. You would be the champion, the face of the lawsuit." Mack said, noting the fading color in Isaiah's face.

Isaiah gave a rueful chuckle as he curled the bill of his cap in his hands again. "I'll definitely be fired now." He looked up.

"It's actually often the opposite," Mack hurried to reassure him. "You're the man who has a lawyer, so if they touch you, I'm here to take off the gloves and add a cause of action for wrongful termination. You have a bubble around you now."

His color came back, and his hands stilled. "Really?"

"Really." Mack nodded once.

"Okay. What's next?" Isaiah asked.

"We need to set up a meeting with some of these other drivers, as many as we can, to get them to sign on to the lawsuit. You start spreading the word among your colleagues, quietly, and we'll set up that meeting.

Let me take down all your contact information and I'll give you a call tomorrow."

Mack scratched down Isaiah's phone number and address. Mack walked him to the door and with a hearty handshake assured Isaiah, "You did the right thing coming here. You and your coworkers need to be treated fairly. I'm looking forward to helping you."

After Isaiah left, Mack turned to his team. Both members were already staring at him expectantly. "Let's order in some lunch and get down to it."

"He has a case?" Gloria asked.

"Yes. Class-action wage violation," Mack said with a grin. "It's going to be a big one."

Mack's new firm had mostly been working small cases since starting up a month ago. A few large ones had followed him from his old position at Myer and O'Toole, but his last big win there—a class-action case—had funded this new firm and his divorce. It was time to start bringing in real money for Poyfair Law Firm, and Isaiah's case could be just what he needed. Class action was something of a specialty of Mack's, and he felt especially confident about the Polson Reed situation.

"What's the company?" asked Antonia.

"Polson Reed Trucking."

"Another trucking company screwing over employees?" Gloria asked.

"Looks like it," he answered.

"How do we start with a class action?" asked Antonia.

Gloria looked at the paralegal. "You start with the company. See if they've been sued before."

"And look into the proper legal name for this particular complaint," added Mack. "Here's his paystub. The issue is, he does work before he starts driving and after he stops driving and they're only paying by the mile. Gloria, you're on case law and researching the judges. We also need to get ahold of employment documents, and make sure they haven't signed anything prohibiting this kind of action."

"And if they did?" Antonia asked.

"Then we'll have to get creative," he answered.

"You have Mr. Garza's information?" Gloria asked.

He handed her the slip of paper and she turned back to her computer.

Mack smirked. "No lunch then?"

"Get me that spicy tuna salad sandwich they have at Specialty's." She was already typing.

Mack turned to Antonia. "And you?"

"I'm not entirely sure what I'm supposed to be doing," she said. "But I'll have the chicken salad sandwich."

"Polson Reed Trucking," Mack said. "Just start with a legal records search on them and then see what you can find on wage laws pertaining to trucking in California and Orange County."

"On it," said Antonia.

"I guess I'll get lunch then," said Mack. He went back to his desk to call in the lunch order at Specialty's Café.

*

Antonia and Gloria had left at a reasonable hour, but Mack had stayed late and he was arriving home in the dark. At work, he knew what he was doing. At his new single-story house, he didn't. It was big enough for the kids to have their own rooms when they stayed with him, but much too empty when they were with their mother. He had bought the house because he needed a place for the kids where they didn't have to be convinced it was fun to camp out in the living room every night. He walked through the white front door and turned on the living room light. It had that smell of "not home," the one that's there until either you assimilate, or the house assimilates to you. He'd been living here for a month now and still, it was not home.

Mack fried an egg and called Melissa.

"I'm just calling to tell Dev and Ava good night," he said.

"They're already in bed, but I'm sure Ava is still reading. Hang on," Melissa said.

Mack glanced at the clock and noted it was a little past ten—later than he had thought.

The conversation with Ava was short, as it always was when her reading was interrupted, and Dev was reported to already be asleep. Melissa said nothing more after the phone was returned to her so Mack told her good night as well. Melissa said, "Yes," and hung up.

Long days had a way of making the mornings feel like they were much further away. Just twelve hours ago, papers had been signed that officially ended their fourteen-year marriage. Mack sat at the small breakfast table and stared out the sliding door to his backyard. Thanks to the darkness beyond, all he saw was his reflection. He rubbed a hand through his hair and turned on the stereo, letting the yacht-rock music fill the house while he ate.

Chapter 2

The initial filing didn't take long with the three members of Poyfair Law devoting most of their time to it. Mack, Antonia, and Gloria were taking calls all week from Isaiah's fellow drivers asking about the lawsuit and what it meant. Antonia booked a conference room at a Holiday Inn Express for a couple weeks out, and they tried to coordinate with the drivers' schedules as much as possible. Then, Isaiah called on Friday.

"They're trying to get us to sign releases. They're offering five hundred bucks to any driver who signs their release and refuses to sign with you," he said.

Mack's chest tightened and he gripped the phone a little harder. He wasn't expecting opposition quite so early in the game. "Don't worry about it, Isaiah," Mack assured him. "It's not going to affect the case."

"What happens if I'm the only one who doesn't sign their release? Class action means a whole bunch of people. It can't just be me."

"It won't be," said Mack. "You'll see at the meeting. Let your fellow drivers know that five hundred is nothing compared to what they're owed. Could you send a copy of that release over? I'd like to see what it says."

"I'll try."

They said good-byes and Mack hung up. "Shit," he said.

Antonia looked up from her work. "What's up?"

"Polson Reed has people signing releases stating they won't be a part of the lawsuit." Mack ran a hand through his hair and stood up. "They're trying to take us out before we even start."

"What kind of release is it?" asked Gloria.

"He's going to try to send a copy of it over," answered Mack.

"In the meantime," said Gloria, "we should move the meeting up if we can. If they're getting employees to sign away their involvement in this case, we need to get them signing on to the case. There's no class action without a class of people behind it."

"Right, okay," said Mack. "Antonia, will you please try to reschedule the meeting? Move it up to next week if you can." He looked to Gloria. "I have to go to Ava's soccer game. If that copy of the release arrives while I'm gone, take a look at it and see what you can figure out. I want to know if this thing is going to be a real problem. Isaiah said they're offering people money to sign it."

Gloria raised an eyebrow. "Cash in hand is awfully tempting."

"Indeed," he said. "That meeting is our best shot at getting things moving before Polson Reed buys out all our plaintiffs."

Mack's mind tumbled through the facts and landed on the concept that this case was supposed to be the launch for Poyfair Firm. They needed something to get their name out there. He couldn't stand on the shoulders of his old firm forever, hoping someone else would seek him out the way Isaiah had. Maybe it was rash of him to start pinning his hopes on this case already, but class-action cases were his strength, and to have one walk in through his office door seemed like an affirmation this firm was going to succeed.

"Hey," said Antonia, snapping him out of his tense reflection. "It's time to go to Ava's soccer game. We'll see you Monday."

*

Mack dreaded going to the soccer game only because of Melissa. It wasn't that things were on bad terms between them, necessarily, but every encounter with her reminded him that not everything worked out, and he didn't need that reminder right now. Still, he was happy to go for Ava, and Dev would be there too. He arrived at the game and didn't quite know whether to sit near Melissa and Dev or give them their space. It was these simple uncertainties he found so taxing now. He struggled inwardly to determine the right course of action.

Screw it. He approached Dev on the bleachers and sat one row below.

"Dad!" Dev exclaimed and moved down to sit next to him. "I got all my multiplication tables perfect today. All the way up to twelve!"

"That's awesome, bud," Mack said. He looked over his shoulder and offered Melissa a close-lipped smile. "Hi," he said.

She returned the smile briefly and nodded. Then she focused her gaze ahead at the field where Ava and her teammates were warming up. Mack followed her lead.

"What else did you do at school today?" Mack asked his son.

Dev started to talk of playing kickball at recess and a friend of his who had the latest racing game.

Dev had a birthday coming up and although Mack and Melissa had raised their kids not to ask for toys or games, the two had their subtle ways of specifying their desires.

Mack listened and loved every moment of his son's undivided attention, but when the game started, his focus shifted to his other child. Mack didn't think Ava would keep up with soccer as she moved into teenhood in the next couple years. She had joined because her friends played, but her interest was clearly waning. When she moved up to the middle school in a couple years, she'd have more people to befriend and likely more who shared her actual interests. She was a bookworm, and she seemed to enjoy running. She certainly seemed to enjoy the running aspect of soccer more than the actual game. Mack could see her going out for track and field. Then again, he could also see her leaving behind anything competitive and choosing instead to run for the pleasure of it and nothing more. Dev, on the other hand, was competitive, but in the world of games and trivia. He was always full of "Did you know...?" quizzes and was disappointed if Mack, Melissa, or Ava did in fact already know the answer to one of his questions. The boy loved nothing more than to tell people new things. When they used to speculate together about what their children might grow up to do, Melissa had said Dev would be a teacher. Mack had always doubted that, thinking Dev's desire to know more than everyone else would lead him into something with more research, or turn him into a winning game show contestant.

Conversations between Melissa and Mack still revolved around the kids, but now with a more pragmatic focus than a whimsical one.

Mack cheered his daughter on and resisted checking his phone until the half-time break. There was a text from Gloria telling him she'd emailed him a scanned copy of the release. Hurriedly, he opened it and skimmed the document.

It was a 1542 release, something so broad it could cripple the case before it even got off the ground. It would be nearly impossible to invalidate. Mack fired back a text, asking Gloria to help Antonia move the meeting up: *We're in a race now,* he typed.

*

They managed to find eleven drivers in addition to Isaiah who could attend a meeting the following Wednesday. The conference room was set up with coffee and doughnuts, and the drivers clustered together in small groups. Antonia was mingling among them, chatting away. She had already built some connections among the men and women after speaking to them on the phone. It never took her long to forge a bond; that was one of the skills that made Mack happy to take her on as a paralegal.

When it seemed all were present, Mack called everyone to have a seat around the table. Caps came off heads and Styrofoam coffee cups settled on the pale fake wood of the boardroom table.

"Many of you know Antonia and Gloria from your phone conversations," he started. "I am Mack Poyfair and we are your legal team. A couple weeks ago, Isaiah brought to my attention that Polson Reed Trucking is not treating their drivers as they should, specifically, not paying you all as they should. I have seen this sort of thing before with Ecklehurst Trucking, if any of you are familiar with that case. It comes down to the fact that you are not being paid for all your work. Your non-driving time is still valuable and it is still time the company is using, so you should be compensated for that. I'm going to break down the Ecklehurst case for you so you can see how this is going to go and then, Gloria and I want to hear your stories."

Mack noted the wariness on the faces of those sitting around the table, so he started with the winnings of the Ecklehurst case. Numbers like

$1.2 million often helped keep a potential plaintiff listening long enough to make a truly informed decision.

"This case was a big deal here in California because it set the standard for how truck drivers should be paid, and that standard is not being upheld by Polson Reed. From what I've seen, I think we're looking at something even bigger for all of you. Federal law says a company can average the compensation for a day as long as it is more than minimum wage. California law, however, mandates that every minute must be paid separately. Winning this case won't be like winning the lottery, but you could get a few thousand to tens of thousands per person."

"What do we have to do exactly?" asked a man to Mack's left. He had a sleeve of black tattoos down one arm, a jungle of leaves and animal faces.

Mack gestured to his right. "Isaiah here is your class representative, meaning he'll be the example for all of you and any other Polson Reed drivers who sign on. You will all have to be deposed at some point. Basically, you'll just answer some questions. It's not necessarily easy, but Antonia, Gloria, and I will help you. We'll prepare you. We're also going to need information on your compensation and your shifts and breaks."

"Are we going to have to miss a lot of work for this?" asked a woman with a puff of dark black curls atop her head.

"We will do our best to work around your shifts, so ideally none to very little," answered Mack.

"They're already asking us to sign something not to do this. What are they going to do if they find out we were here? Or if we sign up with you?" the woman prompted. "I have a family to support."

There were murmurs around the table with similar sentiments, some were single parents, some the sole breadwinners, others in situations where both partners were working to stay afloat.

"The five hundred bucks not to sign with you is worth more with a job than this lawsuit if we lose our jobs," said another man.

"They cannot fire you because of this lawsuit. If they do, that gives us another cause for action against them," Gloria said.

"What if we lose?" This man had spotty facial hair and a potbelly. "I have this cousin who was in on a lawsuit like this four years ago. They lost and ended up paying their own employers."

Mack's spine tingled. "That was before the Ecklehurst case. Ecklehurst set a precedent for how truckers need to be paid. I am confident we are going to win. We have the evidence right now to show that Polson Reed's compensation plan is illegal in the state of California." Mack met the man's eyes and then scanned the room. "What we go after next is class certification, which basically means we say you all are a good representation of all the other truckers in the company. We convince the judge it is better to hear one class-action suit rather than hundreds of individual labor disputes." He didn't mention that if this class action was denied, they could still go forward with any individual who signed on as a plaintiff. Putting doubts in their minds wouldn't help anyone right now and either way, things would shake out in the favor of anyone who joined.

"This case is going to proceed. There's power in numbers. If you sign on to be a part of it, you make the case stronger and you're not going to be fired or given bad shifts or be pushed around because any attacks by them just add to our complaint. If you don't, well, then that's your choice, but you'll be missing out on what's owed to you, and you will still be seen as the enemy by the higher-ups at Polson Reed."

Mack gave them a moment to sit on that information. "You're all here because you've been treated poorly, and you know it. You need to be paid for your work appropriately and legally. The by-the-mile payment system doesn't take into account you doing your vehicle inspection. It doesn't take into account you getting your keys and reports. It doesn't take into account you waiting on the employees at the convenience store to be ready for unloading. The more information I've gotten from Isaiah, and the more I get from you, the clearer it becomes that Polson Reed is short-changing all of you and using a compensation plan that is unfair and illegal. What I'm suggesting you do is tell them to correct that." He paused again. "Antonia has the papers for each of you to sign on as a plaintiff. We'll take a little break here and you can do that with her. Then, we'll start talking next steps."

Mack went to get himself a cup of coffee and surreptitiously observed the room. The truckers were chatting amongst themselves. Several were inching toward Isaiah. After fifteen minutes, Mack had managed to get all their names and they had all been to see Antonia. He breathed a sigh of relief over his cup of coffee and called everyone back to the table.

"I'm glad to have you all on board. We're going to need information from all of you regarding your pay and breaks and everything, but right now, I want to talk more about depositions. Now, I know you all are probably a bit nervous about that, but we're going to be deposing the other side as well. What I need from you now is an idea of the people at Polson Reed, managers or anyone who should be making sure you get paid correctly. I want to know who is going to be honest and who is going to be shady?"

The drivers looked at each other and shoulders started shrugging. Mack looked down at some notes Antonia had gathered on Polson Reed and said, "How about Michael Norman? He's a manager, right?"

There was a snort. "You gotta watch him," said the man with the sleeve tattoo—Luca, as Mack now knew from the break. "He'll weasel his way out of any tight spot."

Mack nodded. "That's great to know." He made a notation next to Michael Norman's name. "We've got Trent Mortinson down here too. What can you tell me about him?"

"He's a company man all the way," said Amanda, the woman with the hair puff. "He would live and die for Polson Reed." She shook her head, conveying just how foolish she thought that was.

Mack wrote that down too. "What do you think of Brian Ivers?"

"Real honest guy. Not sure he could tell a lie if his life depended on it," said a young man. Barry, Mack recalled. "Christine asked him what he thought of her new haircut once and he turned fifteen shades of red before squeaking out, 'unique' and running from the room." There was some laughter around the table.

"That's good." Mack starred Brian Ivers's name. "How about Paul Bender?"

"He's management now," said Kiran, the man with the potbelly, "but he was a driver like us before that. Used to gripe about trying to live on the paycheck himself."

"That's excellent," Mack said. He starred Paul's name as well.

The conversation went on like this for a while, with Mack prompting and the drivers responding with gut-reactions or detailed stories exemplifying character. Eventually, they started voluntarily offering up names and Mack took notes.

By the end of the meeting, everyone seemed more confident. Mack knew there would be ebbs and flows with these clients. They'd feel certain one moment and would find themselves in doubt the next. He encouraged them to call the firm any time they had a question.

"We'll be staying in touch, and you all just need to keep doing your jobs as you do," he said. "When we have meetings, I encourage you to attend as many as possible, but you'll always be kept informed as to how the case is progressing. Thank you all for coming tonight."

After the last driver left the conference room, Mack turned to his team. "That was good. We have twelve representatives. How many drivers in total are there at Polson Reed?"

"We're looking at a class of around six hundred," said Gloria.

Mack felt the surge of victory run through his veins.

"What's next?" Antonia asked.

"Determine all the ways Polson Reed is mistreating their drivers."

Chapter 3

The next day, Gloria and Mack were at their desks poring over the statements provided by the various drivers from last night's meeting. Antonia was out meeting with others to sign retainers.

Gloria approached his desk. "Hey Mack, it seems these drivers weren't always getting their rest breaks and meal breaks," she said. She held out a stack of paystubs and driving logs.

"Really?" Mack took the papers and skimmed highlighted portions. "We can add that to our complaint then. That's a lot of unpaid time. Pre-shift, post-shift, rest, and meal breaks."

Antonia swept into the office, and approached Mack's desk, crushing papers between her hands. "I think I found a problem."

"What sort of problem?" Gloria asked.

Antonia passed Mack the papers. "This is a driver employment contract from Polson Reed. Barry Beady sent it over along with all his paystubs for as long as he's worked there. Anyway, um, there's an arbitration clause in there." She reached across the desk and pointed to a section of the contract. Gloria craned her neck to read the clause at the same time as Mack. If the court upheld that clause, there could not be a class-action lawsuit.

"That's not good," said Gloria. "This case is already over."

"Not so fast," Mack said. He scratched behind his ear, a thought building. "How much do you know about PAGA?"

"The Private Attorneys General Act?" Gloria's lips shifted to one side. "Basically, our drivers would act as attorneys general. They could sue Polson Reed on behalf of all the other employees for labor code violations. We don't need class certification for that."

"Nope," Mack said, leaning back in his chair. "The arbitration clause wouldn't matter. Plus, this would also get around their 1542 releases for anyone who wanted to join us."

"Doesn't most of the money go to the State though?"

"Yes, but our fees would be paid, and the drivers would get something. Plus, it would force a policy change at Polson Reed."

"You think we can use that here?" Antonia asked.

"I think so." He pointed to Gloria. "If they weren't providing meal breaks, as you said, we're looking at a two-hundred-dollar fine per day per driver over several years," Mack said. "Plus, if we're successful, the firm would receive attorney's fees."

"I thought we were doing class action," Gloria said. "PAGA isn't class action."

Mack leaned forward. "Exactly. It'll be a two-part attack. We start with the class action for unfair business practices under business professionals code seventeen-two hundred. If our class certification falls through, we'll go after penalties for each break and every instance of unpaid time for every employee using PAGA."

"So we're going to force a trial?" Gloria asked.

"Yes," he said. "We're taking this to court, one way or another."

"This would be our first trial without the old firm backing us up," Gloria said. Tiny lines sprouted between her eyebrows.

"There had to be one eventually," Mack said. He smiled, but he felt a shiver of risk run down his spine again. It was an unusual strategy and one he had never used before. "Start preparing a federal class-action complaint."

*

Mack picked his kids up from school later that day. Dev spouted fact after fact from the back of the Volvo. In a break from his seemingly endless stream of speech, Mack asked Ava what she was reading.

"*In Search of the Black Rose.* It's a Nancy Drew book," she said, not looking up.

In general, Ava did not like to be interrupted while reading and she was not very tolerant of it on bad days. Today must have been a good one at school because she didn't bite his head off or completely ignore him. Teenhood was creeping up on her and sometimes Mack was forced to notice it.

At the house, the kids dropped their backpacks and shoes by the door and went immediately for the refrigerator, taking out pudding cups and juice boxes—things Mack regularly included in his shopping list now, along with fruit snacks and various flavored crackers and cereals. During his marriage to Melissa, she had done most of the shopping and had been the one adding the kids' snacks to the grocery list. Mack had been the taxi. Division of duties. The dividing is probably what led to them fighting all the time. Neither had felt like they were being appreciated for their contributions to the home and the family. Now, taking care of separate homes and caring for the children as individuals on their own time, the contributions were clear enough, or at least assumed.

Mack sat down at the small table with his kids. Dev was on a geology kick and was currently sharing everything he knew about volcanoes. Ava had her book spread open on the table with one hand while she absently scooped pudding into her mouth with the other, carefully leaning away from the book so as not to drop any on the pages. It was a library book and Ava had always taken great care with them, something her mother had instilled in her with a single joke. When Ava was around six, she had dripped ice cream on a book. Since it was a children's book with shiny pages, it was cleaned up easily enough, but Melissa had told her that the library police would put a black spot on her library card and might not let her take any more books home. It had been a joke, but it had obviously lingered in Ava's mind. Mack couldn't help but wonder what off-hand jokes or comments he might have made in the kids younger years that could affect aspects of their personalities now or later.

When they finished their snacks, Mack told them to do some homework. He opened up his briefcase and pulled out his own homework. They needed to file the Garza et al vs. Polson Reed case as soon as possible. Those 1542 releases were still going around, and it was crucial for the class action that they get ahead of Polson Reed.

With no accountant on staff, Mack was crunching some numbers himself. He'd have to finance this case. At his previous firm, it had been standard for the partners to share in the risk by using their homes as collateral on a line of credit. Defense firms could get lines of credit without putting themselves at risk, but this was the downside of fighting for plaintiffs. There was no consistent stream of income from big companies keeping you on retainer for every legal bump in the road. Gloria and Antonia needed to be paid regularly and he was running low on the funds that had launched Poyfair Law Firm. He made an appointment with his banker for the following Monday.

Mack started supper while Ava returned to her book and Dev turned on the Wii to hit some virtual baseballs. Mack hadn't done much cooking in the years of his marriage, though he would handle a few meals, mostly on the weekends. Since being on his own for the last couple years, he'd rediscovered some old favorites from his pre-Melissa days, and tonight he was making eggplant lasagna—a recipe taught to him by a vegetarian ex-girlfriend in college. He had roasted the eggplant and made the ricotta filling the day before, so it was just a matter of assembling and baking.

As he layered eggplant planks over pasta sauce, he turned the case over in his mind. It had 'win' written all over it, given the ground-breaking Ecklehurst case. The right judge would be key, though. Someone too conservative might just turn this obvious win into a battle.

*

When Mack sliced into the lasagna to dish up Dev's portion, Dev said, "Magma and lava are two different things. It's magma when it's inside the volcano and then it becomes lava when it's outside the volcano."

"How dumb to have two different words for the same stuff. It's still made of the same stuff; it's just in a different place," said Ava, who had been forced to set her book down for supper.

"It's the same for meteorites or meteoroids," said Dev.

Mack could see the space fascination coming soon. Geological interest inevitably led to wondering about the things beyond Earth.

"Meteoroids turn into meteorites when they land on Earth," Dev said.

"Why can't they just be one thing? Plants are plants whether they are inside or outside," said Ava, pointedly looking at a sad little bamboo plant Gloria had given Mack as a housewarming present.

"But plants are weeds when they grow where you don't want them," said Mack.

"No, plants are always plants. They are just weed plants."

"But you don't call them weed plants; you call them weeds," Mack said. "Many things go by more than one name depending on their circumstances. Including people. You call me 'dad,' but I'm also Mack Poyfair."

"We call you dad because you changed, not because your location changed."

While fundamentally his DNA had not shifted—in the same way a meteoroid and meteorite had the same chemical makeup—he could not disagree with his daughter. He absolutely had changed the moment she was born, and he had shifted again with the birth of Dev. "I concede," he said to her.

"It's dumb to have two names for the same stuff in different places."

"I don't!" protested Dev. Mack smiled. "You know more about the thing using one word and you don't have to explain it all. It's easier for scientists to record 'magma' or 'lava' than it is to record 'magma inside the volcano' and 'magma outside the volcano.' It's easier," Dev explained.

Mack nodded to his son. "He has a point. It is more efficient for note-taking to have one word represent the entire concept than it is to have to use a whole string of words."

"What's 'efficient' mean?" asked Dev.

"It means getting things done with less work or less time," Mack said.

Some parents might have seen this argument between the kids as something to settle, but Mack enjoyed it when they debated. Their total devotion to their own perspectives was a trait he shared. Perhaps one that had fed many disagreements with Melissa, but it was also the one that had brought him career success. Still, one thing fighting with Melissa had taught him was that agreeing to disagree on less important matters was crucial. You could never convince everyone of all your beliefs and believing your personal understanding of the world was the only correct one was certainly too much pride to allow for success in anything—work or relationships.

The kids had continued debating through his ruminations and now Mack said, "You can both have your own opinions without needing the other to agree. The topic is not one with an undeniable fact."

Ava and Dev stopped arguing then and finished eating.

*

The remainder of the week, Poyfair Law Firm prepared the complaint and filed it. Although the accusations were about State laws, the dollar amounts they were discussing put it over five million, and that allowed the defendants to have the case removed to federal court. They were now waiting for judge assignment. That weekend Mack and the kids were at a park that had a soccer net. Mack was up against both his kids. Despite the fact that he kept in relatively good shape with morning jogs, the youthful energy of his children had him beaten.

"Hello," called a familiar voice from the side of the net. Mack looked and Ava scored another goal on him.

It was Isaiah.

"Hi," Mack greeted him, reaching out for a handshake. He called his kids over. "Ava, Dev, this is Isaiah Garza. I'm working on a case for him."

"Hi," the two chorused. Ava glanced at Mack and at his nod, she ran after the soccer ball, Dev following. Isaiah gestured behind him to the swing set. "That's my family—Olivia and Matthew."

Mack took in the petite woman pushing a little boy in the toddler swing. He looked to be around four years old. Both had dark hair and wide smiles.

"We've got a second one coming in four months."

"Congratulations," Mack said.

Isaiah cleared his throat. "I saw you over here and I didn't want to interrupt your family time or anything, but…how's it going? With the case."

Mack gave him a comforting smile. "We've filed. Now we're waiting for judge assignment and then we see what the judge says about our causes of action."

"What does that mean? What could the judge say?"

"Basically, they will say yes or no regarding our complaints. It's whether they agree that the laws we say are being broken actually may have been broken based on the information we gave them."

Isaiah's brow furrowed. "You mean it could all get thrown out and the case goes nowhere?"

"I don't think that's likely."

"But there's no guarantee that it will go forward?"

"I can't guarantee anything, but it all looks really good to me," said Mack.

"Tell me what's in the way," said Isaiah, his stance widening. "Tell me what obstacles we are facing."

It was becoming quite clear that Isaiah took his role as a leader very seriously. Mack scratched behind his ear. "Look, the Ecklehurst case does set a precedent, but it was only a district court opinion so it's not like another court needs to follow it. We've got the 1542 releases working against us and we are doing something sort of unusual with PAGA." Isaiah nodded, having had a long conversation with Gloria earlier in the week regarding the use of PAGA. "Also…" Mack hesitated. He didn't want this next part to sound like he was blaming Isaiah for anything. "You signed an arbitration clause with Polson Reed."

Isaiah paled a little. "So I can't sue them?"

"The judge could dismiss our case and uphold that clause," Mack admitted. He glanced behind him to see Ava and Dev facing off over the soccer ball.

"So this could go nowhere?"

"There are ways around it," Mack said. "Arbitration clauses are meant to prevent class action, but we're going in with more than just a class action. It will all be fine, Isaiah." Mack clapped him on the shoulder.

"Polson Reed is definitely taking advantage of you and your colleagues, and they will be held accountable for it. I am certain. Now, go enjoy your Saturday with your lovely family."

Isaiah nodded but his face did not reflect as much confidence as Mack had hoped to impart. Mack had very little doubt about this case proceeding, whether it would come out in their favor or not... That was always uncertain. It was impossible to say which way a case like this would go until he knew what he was up against. The first piece of the puzzle would be knowing which judge was assigned.

Dev pulled Mack from his work thoughts by suggesting they switch to the basketball court. That was more Mack's wheelhouse anyway. The kids always easily trounced him in soccer.

*

When Mack came into the office the next morning, he went straight to his desk to see if there was any news on the judge assignment. There was. He opened the envelope and skimmed down to the pertinent information. *Not conservative. Not conservative*, he mentally chanted. The first piece of the puzzle slid into place and the picture was not what Mack had been hoping for.

Chapter 4

"Judge Marcus Keats," Mack said, dropping the notice onto Gloria's desk. "Could we have drawn a worse judge for this case?"

Gloria looked it over and made a face. "Not that I'm aware of."

Mack drew a hand roughly through his hair. Marcus Keats's career as a lawyer had involved working on oil spills, on the side of the oil companies, and he had been alarmingly good at it.

"I take it he is conservative?" asked Antonia from her desk.

"There isn't a judge in the state of California who's more conservative," said Gloria.

Antonia's ever-smiling mouth stretched into a sympathetic line.

Mack scooped up the notice and went back to his own desk. Upon logging into his email, he found a message from a firm called Monroe Casper. A quick search of the name revealed they were from Ohio and were top lawyers from top schools. The email stated they would be defending Polson Reed.

"You have got to be kidding me," Mack said. "Gloria, Antonia, we have opposing counsel. Monroe Casper out of Ohio."

"Polson Reed is based out of Ohio," Antonia volunteered.

"I looked them up," he said, brushing a hand through his hair. "Polson Reed isn't kidding around with this lawsuit. Monroe Casper mean the big guns."

"They're trying to intimidate us into settling for a smaller sum," said Gloria, leaning back in her desk chair. "They're giving us an unknown opponent to throw us off kilter."

Mack agreed with her assessment. It wasn't ideal to be facing counsel from out of state, especially ones of such high caliber. "Let's see that it doesn't do that," Mack said. He checked his watch and rose from his desk. "I have a meeting at the bank. I'll be back in an hour or so. I don't care who we're up against. We'll do battle against the best they have." Over the last year, Mack had become very adept at confident statements, even when he felt uncertainty. It wouldn't make things easier to face unknown counsel through this ever-growing case, but it did mean Poyfair Law Firm probably had something strong to go on.

*

Despite being plagued by doubts now that he knew he was up against the most conservative judge in the state, Mack needed to project confidence in this case. He stood in the waiting area of the bank and sipped on a cup of coffee. He needed to secure the line of credit for Poyfair Law if this case was going to go anywhere at all. Mack had a long-standing good relationship with Elena Williams, his banker for the last twenty years or so. When she came out to the waiting area to retrieve him, they shook hands amicably.

"How are the kids?" she asked.

"Doing well. Dev's on geology now. Ava is tearing through the Nancy Drew books."

"I remember those," said Elena as she settled behind her desk. "I had a whole collection of them.

"How can I help you today, Mack?" she asked.

"I need to open a line of credit for Poyfair Law Firm. You should have all the paperwork," he said. "I have a house to put up as collateral."

"I see," she said. "How much credit are you hoping to have?"

"Eight hundred thousand," Mack said.

Elena's eyebrows flicked up ever so slightly. "We'll need to see a valuation of your house to determine if it is worth that."

"Of course," Mack said. "We've just landed a rather large class-action lawsuit against Polson Reed Trucking."

"Oh?" Elena prompted. "You're starting to specialize a little, aren't you?"

Mack chuckled. "I suppose so. We've got a few other cases going, but this one is going to be big, and expensive."

"Tell me more about it," she said.

Mack told her about the potential number of clients and the violations they had pinpointed.

"Now tell me about your new house," Elena prompted.

Mack did that too and offered up the paperwork he had on it from the recent purchase.

"Well Mack," she said, "this all looks pretty good. I think we'll be able to work out something. It might not be as high as you were hoping, however."

"I understand," he said. "We just need something to help us move forward. When we win this case, it's going to take care of things."

When Mack signed the papers later, he took a deep breath. It was just a line of credit and he hadn't spent any of it, so technically, he was not yet in debt. He had done this before with the old firm but doing it on his own was much scarier. This was his home and his law firm, and it was Antonia and Gloria's jobs. He squared up his shoulders and signed. It was simple: He needed the capital to proceed, so he could move forward on the case without worrying about the firm's finances.

*

Isaiah was frequently in touch, and obviously felt the strain of having gotten his coworkers into this with him. Isaiah was impatient for progress reports. Mack explained that there was a lot of waiting involved in the early stages. Right now, they were waiting for Polson Reed's answer to their filed complaints. It took over two weeks.

"What the hell is this supposed to mean?" Mack asked after looking over the thirty-page brief that had arrived by mail that morning.

They weren't just denying the complaint, they were claiming the entire case was invalid.

"What's up?" asked Gloria, approaching his desk after hearing his exclamation.

"They filed a 12(b)(6)," he said. "They're saying the case has no legal merit whatsoever."

"How do they figure that?"

Mack handed her the brief and pointed to a particular line. "They're citing the Federal Aviation Administration Authorization Act."

"Polson Reed is a trucking company," she said. "What does aviation have to do with it?"

"I don't know," he answered. I'm not familiar with that Act. Can you head over to the research library this afternoon and figure out what it means and why they think it should apply to a trucking company?"

"Sure thing."

Just then Mack's phone rang, displaying Isaiah as the caller. As much as he didn't want to answer it, now that he knew Polson Reed felt they could dismiss the case entirely, Mack wanted to keep Isaiah reassured.

"Hello?" he answered.

"Hi Mack, it's Isaiah."

"Hi Isaiah. How are you doing today?" Mack asked.

"All right. I'm just calling to check-in since it's my day off," he said.

Mack scrubbed a hand through his hair. "We were waiting on that answer from Polson Reed's attorneys," he hedged.

"Did it come?"

"An answer came, but we've got to work out some finer points with them," he said.

"What was the answer? What points?" pressed Isaiah.

There was a common misconception among clients, mostly thanks to TV and movies, that lawyers stored every piece of legislation and legal ruling ever made in their brains and could recognize and understand every legal precedent and law they were presented with on demand. Mack pressed the heel of his hand to his forehead, trying not let it fall into folds. "They're trying to deny that the case has legal grounds. They think they can get out of it by applying a federal act that deals with aviation." His words were selected carefully to imply that the opposing firm was making futile efforts.

"But we're drivers, not pilots," said Isaiah.

"Exactly," Mack said.

"That seems like a stupid thing to try on their part."

Mack didn't want to disabuse him of this notion. But just because a law seemed to apply to only one segment of industry didn't mean it could not be used in others. "We're getting it sorted out," said Mack. "I've got to run. You enjoy your day off."

Isaiah didn't seem entirely reassured by this, but he said, "Okay. Good-bye."

*

When Gloria returned from the library later that afternoon, Mack sat down with her to get her breakdown of the FAAAA.

"So F Quad-A was passed in 1994, and it is about travel across state lines. Monroe Casper is trying to say that it should apply to truck drivers, since they travel between states. Basically, it says that only federal law applies because the business requires crossing state lines." Gloria handed him some photocopied pages with her highlights and notes. "Under federal law, there's no requirement for breaks or for pre-shift or post-shift compensation," she added.

"I'm aware of that, thanks," Mack said, barely managing not to snap at her. Monroe Casper was proving to be a pain in the ass.

"Now before you get all bothered about it, I found something to dispute it." Gloria reached over and slid some papers out of the way, pointing to a particular section she had highlighted in green.

Gloria had found a case where dump truck drivers had brought a suit against their company, which tried to reject it using the FAAAA. As Mack pored through the pages detailing that case, he saw the possibilities. They had claimed their right to pre-shift compensation through the prevailing wages theory.

"If these guys got pre-shift pay while doing government driving, then there's no reason our drivers shouldn't get their compensation for pre-shift and post-shift work. Also, according to the California labor codes, these drivers should be getting meal breaks and rest breaks and those laws should apply for the safety of the public," said Mack.

"FAAAA preempts if the law affects the employer's prices, services, or routes," Gloria said, playing Devil's advocate.

"Breaks are a public safety issue when it comes to truck drivers," Mack said. "Nobody wants eighty thousand pounds of steel being driven sixty miles an hour by somebody who's nodding off."

Gloria smiled, and the two began to prepare their own brief, focusing on the precedent of the dump truck case as well as California's regulations regarding rest and meal breaks.

*

The coming weeks found Poyfair Law Firm preparing for partial judgment with Judge Keats. They sent along their own brief in response and finally met in Judge Keats's chambers. Gloria and Mack took their seats after formally meeting Harry Clark and Meghan Moore of Monroe Casper Law Firm. Harry Clark had thick silver hair and a suit that screamed power. Meghan Moore's blonde hair was in a sleek ponytail. Everything about the team projected surety.

Judge Keats steepled his fingers with his elbows resting on his desk. "Mr. Poyfair," he began, "I have come to the conclusion that the meal breaks, and rest breaks, are indeed tied to the prices, routes, and services. When they have to provide a meal or rest break, they may decide to alter a route or have that route through a different state. The FAAAA helps regulate the industry and is applicable. With that understanding, I'm afraid you have no claim for the rest and meal breaks."

Mack felt his stomach drop out. *Shit. This case can't be over.* Resisting the urge to rise from his chair, Mack leaned forward. "Your Honor, let's just think this all the way through. Even if you agree that these meal and rest break laws are not the same as Labor Code 226 claims, requiring separate compensation for non-driving time, the labor code also specifically addresses the timing and imposition of meal and rest breaks. They've made an argument, which I disagree with completely, but they've said it's impracticable in their industry. We can all agree that general principles of employment law are not preemptive. California passes a law saying you can't sexually harass your employees, and sexual harassment training and violations could drive up the price. Different states have different harassment laws. Could the defendant come in and say that FAAAA preempts it? We can't go that far. You can't possibly say that the FAAAA applies to every California law. Trucking companies must comply with many state laws concerning environmental regulations, speed limits, and loading zones. Those things also cost the company money to comply with, and that cost affects the price of their services."

Judge Keats looked uncertain, and Mack went on.

"Before these drivers start driving, they're getting reports together, they're checking over their truck. Imagine if you have a nine-to-five and you have to come in thirty minutes early to turn on your computer, assemble reports, and have a pre-call with somebody before your day actually starts, before you actually clock in. All that work is for the benefit of the employer. That's essentially what these drivers are doing. Their routes are set for a certain time, but they have to show up an hour before that to complete pre-shift work—checking tires, measuring fluid levels, and the whole pre-shift inspection of the truck. These are hours worked and they need to be compensated for it."

"Well," said Keats, but Mack kept going.

"And they go through a whole other set of tasks like that when they get back, plus they need to clean out their cabin to prepare it for the next driver. None of these individual tasks take very long and they aren't overly difficult, but five minutes there and ten minutes here, Your Honor, and they're missing out on an hour's worth of pay every shift."

"Mr. Poyfair," Keats said, "if you will please."

Mack realized he had risen to his feet sometime during his energetic speech and now resumed his seat.

"I will take this all under submission," Judge Keats said.

*

Back at the office, Gloria and Mack filled Antonia in on the proceedings.

"That's great. You got him to think about it!" she enthused, ever the positive one in the office.

Gloria snorted. "Would have been better if he had just ruled in our favor to begin with."

"He's considering it. This case is still happening," Mack insisted.

"We'll see," said Gloria.

Chapter 5

*E*very email received in the coming weeks was fraught with tension for Mack. He had taken out the line of credit thinking this battle wouldn't be a particularly long one, and that the funds his firm won would easily pay back whatever was owed on the line of credit. He wasn't in for much yet and the whole case could be thrown out with a single email, but he was hoping this would be the case to really make a name for Poyfair Law. If the case did get accepted, though, Mack was starting to see a long battle ahead. If Polson Reed's lawyers were going to try to reject everything, it was clear they were in this to fight every step of the way and would not sweep the complaints away with an upfront settlement.

In the meantime, Mack and his team were working on other cases in conjunction with other firms. A paycheck was finally coming in from one of them. Mack had been in on this case for a couple years, but his share of the awarded attorney's fees came out to only $225,000. At least it was something to keep the firm afloat and keep the Polson Reed case moving forward, and it reminded Mack that he only needed one complaint approved to get the case in front of a jury. Even if Judge Keats threw out the meal and rest breaks, there was the pre-shift and post-shift work. If only that could go through, it would be a victory. Polson Reed would have to defend themselves.

Mack told Isaiah he would call again when they had new information but reminded him that courts are slow, and it could be months before they knew where they stood.

Mack took the kids out to Disneyland one weekend amid the long, stressful wait for Judge Keats's ruling. With the theme park so close, Melissa and Mack purchased annual passes to take the kids. The sheer insanity of the place provided a decent distraction for Mack. He needed to find a way out of the workspace in his head, and the noise and calamity of hundreds of kids seeing Mickey was certainly one way to do it, albeit not the doctor-recommended method.

Later that evening Melissa called to wish the kids good-night. They spoke with enthusiasm about their day at the park. Mack did his best not to listen in as the kids chatted with their mother, but it was clear they were talking about their day. Mack was surprised when Ava handed the phone back to him. Typically, the kids just hung up when they were done.

"Hello?" he said.

"You took them to Disneyland?" she asked abruptly. "I was going to take them next week with my sister and her kids."

"I don't think they'll mind going two weekends in a row. There's an awful lot to do there," he said. The tone of Melissa's voice spurred him to head into his bedroom so the kids wouldn't overhear. He closed the door behind him and sat on the mussed bed. He never made the bed anymore. Melissa had always wanted it made, so when they'd been together, he'd done it. Now, he only made the bed when the sheets were changed.

"That's not the point," Melissa snapped. "We need to discuss these things."

"You mean you want me to report to you what I plan to do with the kids every time they're with me?" Mack asked. Slight tension crept into his voice.

"If it's something grand, I'd like to know about it," she said.

"You didn't tell me you were planning to take them next week."

"I just did."

Mack said nothing for a beat. He thought the divorce had meant he wouldn't have to fight with her anymore. Generally, they'd mostly been on the same page with the children over the years, but leading separate lives had apparently shifted some things. This didn't seem like a battle worth fighting, considering he couldn't do anything about it after the fact.

"Sorry," he said finally. "Next time, I'll let you know if I have anything in particular planned."

There was a pause on her end now and Mack could imagine her face—caught between wanting to pursue the fight and accepting his apology.

"All right then," she said. "Good-bye."

The connection ended before Mack could say good-bye as well.

In some ways, divorce had simplified things, but in others, it was quite complicated. They hadn't gotten being married right, and now he wondered if they would be bad at divorce as well. He rubbed a hand over his neck and then stood up to rejoin his children in the living room where they were watching *Black Beauty*. It had been Ava's turn to pick the movie. Dev was building with LEGO while the movie played, and Ava told him to stop rummaging through his bin of bricks as the sound overpowered the TV audio.

Mack paused in the hallway to observe his kids for a moment. They couldn't be messing up their divorce too badly if the kids were doing all right. Ava had withdrawn from friends a bit after the initial announcement, and Dev had picked fights with both him and Melissa for a while, until they made it clear that they would not stand for it.

Ava noticed him hovering in the hallway and asked, "What are you doing just standing there?"

"Just watching you two," he said, smiling.

"Weirdo," she said. "Can we have popcorn?"

Mack said yes and went to the kitchen to put a bag of popcorn in the microwave. Dev followed as he liked to watch the bag expand.

"What if it explodes?" Dev asked.

"Then the microwave will be full of popcorn," said Mack.

"One time, in a book, they made so much popcorn it filled a house."

"I remember you telling me that," said Mack.

"It was like a popcorn wave. Did you know a giant wave is a tsunami?" Then he was off, telling Mack everything he knew about waves and water.

*

It was nearly a month before Judge Keats issued his ruling on the complaints of the case. Mack opened the message at his desk and read through it. The meal and rest break claims were not accepted under the FAAAA preemption, but the pre-shift and post-shift time was still on the table. Mack sagged in relief and then straightened up. They had a case now, and that meant the real work was about to begin.

"We're moving forward with pre- and post-shift work on the Polson Reed case," Mack told Gloria and Antonia.

"And the breaks?" asked Gloria.

Mack shook his head. "Off the table."

Gloria nodded as though she had expected this to happen.

"We're moving forward as a collective action with PAGA," Mack said.

"We're not going to try class action first?" Gloria asked.

"There's no point with Keats on this. He's going to uphold that arbitration clause and rather than turn into a nuisance right away, I think we should take the unexpected route. It will put the guys at Monroe Casper on their heels and we will definitely be able to pursue it."

"We'll need to prep all the class representatives for depositions, and we need to prepare for depositions of the Polson Reed higher-ups," said Gloria.

"We're going to need all the employment records for each of our twelve drivers," Mack told Antonia. "From when they first started at Polson Reed to the present. And we need to set up another meeting with all of them. We'll explain how the depositions are going to work and then we'll set up individual meetings to prep them for their depositions with opposing counsel."

Antonia nodded.

"Gloria," he said, "let's prepare an appeal to the Ninth Circuit regarding those meal breaks and rest breaks. Our argument stands, and I think we might have a shot of getting those back into action."

She lifted an eyebrow. "You're not going to let anything go easy for Polson Reed."

"There's no reason I should," he replied.

*

The twelve drivers assembled with the members of Poyfair Law Firm in the Holiday Inn Express conference room again at the end of June. After welcoming everyone, Mack got down to business.

"Since the case is proceeding, you all will be called in for depositions. We're here tonight to start preparing you for those depositions, and we will be setting up individual prep sessions as well once we've had a chance to go over your employment records and see what the defense might come at you with." He observed the stoic faces around the room. If he focused on individuals, signs of anxiety became obvious. Amanda was running her index fingernail across the edge of her thumb. Barry was popping his finger joints. Kiran was scratching behind his ear. These people were accustomed to spending most of their working hours alone, and the idea of confrontation over that work was stress-inducing for them. He had more bad news.

"These depositions are not for your benefit. They are not for you to tell your story. They are all for the defense. Every time one of them asks you a question, he is trying to catch you out and screw you over. You're going to have to be careful about your answers. That's why we need to prep.

"They're going to try to make the situation as intimidating as possible to put you on edge. The depositions will likely be at an office in a high rise with security guards to escort you. They'll be wearing suits and they're going to video record the depositions. My first piece of advice to you: wear a suit or something really sharp. Your Sunday-best. You don't need to go out and buy a suit, but dress like you might for a funeral or a wedding."

"Do we have to do this on our own?" interjected Kiran.

"I will be there with each of you, but I can't answer the questions for you. I won't be saying much of anything. I'm there to make sure they don't ask questions that cross over the line," Mack said. "These depositions will be grueling," he said. "Each of you will likely spend an entire day or more in your deposition. They might try to make it seem like a conversation, like a friendly chat. That's not what it is. You will need to have your guard up and think through your answers carefully." Mack had seen before how a long deposition could make a client forget their instructions. It could be exhausting staying on high alert for eight hours or more. Preparing them as individuals was crucial to preventing that exhaustion from making them crack.

"When we do our prep sessions, you're not going to like me at times," Mack said. "That's the point. I need to help you be ready for all the crap they're going to throw at you."

Barry spoke up. "What do you mean? I thought they had to defend themselves. You're making it sound like we're going to be put in the hotbox and accused of stuff. Like we'll need to defend ourselves."

"Polson Reed's lawyers are going to be looking for ways to discredit you. They'll try to show you aren't a good employee. They'll bring up any time you've done anything wrong. They're going to ask you leading questions, like 'Do you agree that it is important to be on time?' And when you say yes, they're going to follow that up by reminding you of any time you've ever been late that they have a record of. They're also going to ask you why you never recorded your pre-shift and post-shift time if you thought you were entitled to wages for it. But you're all going to be ready for anything they ask you."

"This sounds like a pretty big-time commitment," said Patrick, a driver who had six kids, if Mack remembered correctly.

"You're right," Mack said. "We'll have to do a few prep sessions with each of you and then there will be the actual deposition."

"How many days is this going to take?" he pressed.

"We will work prep sessions around your schedules. As for the actual depositions, we'll see what we can do, but the defense has a big role in that." Mack paused. He didn't want to mislead them, but he also didn't want to scare them off. "You might have to take some time off work for them."

There was some unrest about this, but eventually the room calmed, and everyone was settled enough to schedule their first prep sessions.

Luca approached Mack while others were scheduling with Antonia.

"What happens if I decide to leave Polson Reed while this case is going on?" he asked.

"You'll still be a part of this case," Mack said. "Are you quitting Polson Reed?"

Luca scratched the back of his neck. "Things aren't so good there. There's so much tension between us and everyone else in the company. We're getting crap shifts. I need something reliable for my family's sake, and I just don't feel good about sticking around there. My cousin has his own trucking company and he's got openings. Offered me one."

Mack clapped him on the bicep. "That sounds great. You should do what's best for you and your family. It won't hurt the case to have you change companies."

"The thing is, it might make it hard for me to get time off."

Mack had no doubt the man's cousin would be understanding enough to let his own family have a day off, but if Luca was having doubts about it all, he might become a less active class representative. Mack didn't want that to happen. "Luca, we'll work it all out. Just because you're leaving this company behind doesn't mean they don't owe you for the time you worked for them. Take your new job. Antonia will give you a call to set up prep sessions. You don't need to do it tonight."

Luca nodded and walked away.

*

Depositions were the sticky spot now. Most of the drivers were not the sort to enjoy being put on the spot. This became abundantly clear when the depositions began.

Kiran was first up. Mack gave him a quick reminder that this deposition would be the defense trying to play "Gotcha" and it was Kiran's job to not play into the game. They settled into a conference room in the rented law office in downtown Los Angeles. Mack had been dead-on about Polson Reed's legal team setting it up to be intimidating. They'd had to sign in at the lobby and were escorted up to the fortieth floor by a security guard. The long mahogany table was overkill for the deposition attendees. Kiran had worn his Sunday best, but the plaid pearl-snaps on his dress shirt didn't stand up well against the designer suits of Harry Clark and Meghan Moore. The camera was aimed pointblank at Kiran, and Mack took a seat next to him.

The pep talk he'd given didn't last long in Kiran's mind when Harry Clark started in on the questions.

Things came to a head when Clark asked, "Isn't it *your* responsibility to record your time and ensure your pay is calculated properly?"

Kiran's face drew together in anger. "What do you mean?"

"It's your responsibility to record your time, so if you weren't getting paid for it, why didn't you say something?"

"Are you serious?" Kiran asked. Kiran was among the first to sign up to the case, telling Mack how he'd been complaining about the pay for years. "You all kept records of me being two minutes late to a meeting once and you got no records of me askin' about the pay? They always said, 'That's what you signed up for. It's part of your job. Nobody else is complaining.'"

Clark raised an eyebrow. "Did you keep records of your time? Did you make sure your pay was correct?"

"What a stupid question. I turn in my time logs, but it has to be filled out the way they say it does." Everyone knew the trucking industry had issues with time logs being fudged so drivers could drive as much as the company needed, regardless of the legal limits on how long they were supposed to drive for without a break.

"Are you sure you didn't change some of the numbers on your time log? Maybe lie about the time you worked?"

Kiran rose from his seat. "What are you accusing me of?" Mack put a hand on Kiran's arm, but the man didn't even glance his way. "I am a good driver and I've been driving a long time! I know what I'm doing, you asshole!" Kiran was leaning over the table now.

"It just seems impossible that you could have covered so much ground in such a short amount of time. There are days here that...well, that don't seem to add up." Harry Clark's self-satisfied expression didn't last long.

"You don't know shit!" Kiran made a move to go around the end of the table and Mack stood up.

"Okay, okay," he said, stepping between Kiran and the defense team. "I think we need a break here," he said to Harry Clark. "Kiran will be happy to answer your question after we take a minute." Mack saw Kiran's heaving chest and red face. "How about five? We're just going to step out." Clark gave a nod as though he didn't mind one bit, but Mack had seen him lean away when Kiran approached. Kiran was an intimidating guy at six-foot-five, but if he took a swing at Harry Clark...that could ruin Mack's case.

Mack indicated that Kiran should exit the room first, mostly to keep himself between Kiran and Clark.

In the hall, he addressed Kiran. "We went over this," Mack said. "He is here to get you worked up. He's going to be pushing your buttons. You have a teenager at home, right?"

Kiran nodded.

"Doesn't he ever try to deliberately get under your skin?" Mack asked.

Kiran relaxed into a resigned head tilt.

"You gotta keep your head in there. Answer the questions and stay focused. They sound like they're accusing you of things because they're hoping you did something wrong somewhere along the way. You are a good driver. Don't let them make you doubt that."

Kiran snarled a little but nodded again. "I hear you. I'll get it together."

And he did, well enough to finish it out. The other depositions went similarly over the course of the next few months. Barry threw a box of tissues at Harry Clark who had the good sense to dodge. Patrick pulled the microphone out of the stand and Mack had to intervene before he could lunge across the table to knock Clark over the head with it. Antonia gave him a mug with a referee design on it as a joke. Depo days wore Mack out, and he still had to depo the other side himself.

Chapter 6

"We got Polson Reed's response to our deposition notice," said Gloria.

This was the next big gamble in a class-action lawsuit. Mack and his team couldn't just select who they were going to take depositions from. Instead, they had to submit a deposition notice saying they wanted to depo the person most knowledgeable about the wage practices dealing with pre-shift and post-shift time. Polson Reed and their legal team then designated someone for that. This seemed incredibly unfair to Mack as it usually resulted in the best liar delivering some company lines.

"Who did we get?" he asked.

"Ed Schmidt."

"Do we know anything about him?"

"His name didn't come up with any of the drivers," said Gloria. "Do you want me to schedule his deposition?"

"Yeah. Then see what we can find out about him, personality-wise." Mack had been hoping the assigned person would be a name he knew, one that the drivers had suggested would be reliable, but here they were. Ed Schmidt. "Also, we need to find someone who can crunch all these numbers for us so we can seek penalties through PAGA."

"I might have someone," said Gloria.

"They have to be good," said Mack. Despite the need to run Poyfair Law Firm on a budget for now, he wasn't going to skimp on this critical piece of their case. The right expert witness could make or break a case. It had to be someone who was precise and professional with an unassailable background, who could handle being questioned with grace.

"She's great," Gloria insisted. "Her name is Aubrey Vassos. We did undergrad together. She has a PhD in mathematics now."

"Get her CV and set up a time when I can interview her."

"No problem. She's coming in tomorrow." Gloria drew a sheet of paper out from under her legal pad and handed it to Mack. "She'll be here at two o'clock."

Mack glanced over the CV in his hands. Gloria thinking ahead was part of the reason he'd asked her to join him at Poyfair Law. Her efficiency was unparalleled.

*

The opposition had requested the deposition take place at their local co-counsel's office. It was another large room in a large office building with security sign-ins. It didn't matter to Mack. He was running the show today, and the dark wood furniture and marble floors weren't going make him feel inferior.

Mack immediately disliked the look of Ed Schmidt. He entered the room like he would be the one asking questions. The tall, blond man was fifty percent swagger and fifty percent smirk. He looked slick as hell and about as trustworthy. Mack shook his hand, half expecting it to come away slimy.

Mack opened with some questions about Ed's background with the company.

Eventually, the specifics of the driver payment were broached.

"They're paid by the mile, of course, and"—Mack noted the uptick in Ed's confidence—"there's the route pay."

Mack was tempted to glance Gloria's way to see if this rang any bells for her, but he resisted. The last thing he wanted was to indicate alarm and make Ed feel like he'd put them on their heels. "What is this route pay?" Mack asked.

Ed leaned back in his chair. "It's a specific sum to pay the drivers for the pre-shift and post-shift work time."

A cold sweat populated under Mack's suit jacket. This guy was claiming specific payment for the very thing they were accusing Polson Reed of not compensating employees for. *Shit.* "How is the route pay calculated?"

"It's thirty dollars per shift," he answered.

"And how did you all arrive at that amount?" This had to be made up. This had to be a save-the-company's-skin lie that Ed was told to put forth.

"It's based on a study we did," he said.

"What sort of study?" Mack pressed.

"We figured it out based on our experience. I used to be a driver myself and I've been with Polson Reed for twenty-plus years. We do know a bit about our business, Mr. Poyfair," he mocked. "We figure the pre- and post-shift work is about an hour and half's worth of time and so we calculated the route pay based on our twenty dollar an hour base."

"How did you come to an hour and a half?"

"That's just how long those things should take," he said.

"Did you break it down between pre-shift and post-shift work?"

Ed blinked. "Of course, yeah."

"How much time for pre-shift and how much time for post-shift?" Mack asked. In the same way Harry Clark had tried to catch the plaintiffs out, Mack was determined to work this guy over. This route pay was a devastating curveball and he needed to trip Ed up.

"It was split even. Forty-five minutes each," said Ed.

"How did you determine that? Did you ask drivers how long it took? Did you send out surveys?"

"I don't recall doing any of that. It's all based on my experience. I know how long those things take because I did them until I got moved up to management," he said.

Mack continued to press Ed on all the aspects of this route pay repeatedly. The company man stuck to his lines. Mack was certain he was being lied to, but Ed wasn't tripping over anything he laid out.

"Look, Mr. Poyfair," Ed said finally with an arched brow, "We're already paying these drivers their due. The route pay covers the pre-shift and post-shift. That's all there is to it."

"Mr. Schmidt," said Mack, "did you talk about this deposition with anyone in management at Polson Reed?"

Ed shrugged. "I probably mentioned it."

"What did you talk about?"

Ed met his gaze straight on. "I don't remember." The corners of Ed's mouth ticked up and Mack clenched his teeth.

The deposition wrapped up quickly after that. As soon as he left, Mack turned to Gloria. "We're in the shit now. Where the hell did this route pay business come from? Why haven't we heard about it from the drivers?"

"I have no idea," she replied. "It sounds like an easy out for Polson Reed, but if these drivers are actually getting paid this route pay for the pre-shift and post-shift time, we don't have a leg to stand on."

"If this is for real, why didn't it come up sooner?" Mack asked, raking a hand through his hair.

*

Back at the office, Mack called Isaiah. In an effort not to alarm him, Mack didn't lay out any of Ed's claims about what route pay was for. Instead, he asked the most basic question. "I just had the deposition of Ed Schmidt. He was telling me about route pay. What is that?"

"The route pay?" Isaiah asked.

"Yes. Thirty dollars a day," Mack said, hoping to jog Isaiah's memory without leading it anywhere.

"Right. That," Isaiah said. "A few years back we had a disagreement over salary. We wanted raises and got the union involved. In the end, we didn't get our raises. Instead, they offered us a thirty-dollar bonus per route."

"That's what it is called, a bonus per route?" Mack felt a slight release of the tensed muscles in his neck. This wasn't over yet, but it was clear that Ed and some cronies at Polson Reed had tried to fabricate pay that didn't exist.

"That's what we were told it was," Isaiah said. "What's going on?"

"Ed tried to feed some line about the route pay being compensation for pre-shift and post-shift work," he said. "Clearly they thought they could use that claim to get out of this lawsuit." Mack made his tone dismissive, indicating that he found the ploy stupid. It was anything but stupid if Mack couldn't find the evidence to back up what Isaiah told him. He said good-bye to Isaiah and walked over to Gloria's desk.

"Isaiah told me the route pay was part of a deal worked out with the union when the drivers wanted a raise in salary a few years ago. No mention of pre-shift or post-shift pay," he said.

"I spoke with Amanda," Gloria said. "Sounds like Isaiah had the same response she did. Funny how they were saying it was all exempt under FAAAA before and now it's, 'We are already paying them for that time.'"

"That's exactly what makes this so fishy," Mack said.

"Shall we phone up the others?"

"It can't hurt to verify that they all understand route pay to be the same thing. Make sure none of them have heard it referred to as pre- or post-shift time pay."

They got in touch with the other drivers over the course of the next few days and every one of them confirmed Isaiah's explanation about the route pay. Now it was just a matter of backing up their version with concrete evidence. Judge Keats was likely to side with the employer in a he-said/they-said scenario like this. They needed something to tear down Ed's claims.

"Get a copy of the employee handbook and look through it for any mention of the route pay. We should also get in touch with the union rep. See what they might have documented. Then get Ed Schmidt on the books for another depo," Mack said after he and Gloria compared notes on their phone calls. "I want to see what he has to say about company records for this route pay."

*

Mack and the team spent some time poring over all the employment documents for Polson Reed, searching for any mention of the route pay and its connection to pre-shift and post-shift time. In the 140-page employee handbook, there wasn't a single word about it.

When he was back in a room with Ed, Mack said, "Let's talk about this route pay a little more."

Ed rolled his eyes.

"Was the purpose of the route pay ever put into writing?"

Mack studied Ed carefully, waiting for a response. The man looks up and to the right as though trying to remember. "You know, I don't think so, but it might be."

"Something as important as this isn't written down? Is it in the handbook?" Mack asked. "The last time we spoke, you told me the handbook was a complete document that detailed compensation. Can you show me that section?" Mack passed Ed a copy of the handbook. Meghan Moore leaned forward to get a look at it and then settled back into her chair.

Ed flipped open the handbook and found the ten-page section on compensation.

Mack stretched across the table to point to the handbook. "Show me where it says route pay is separate compensation for the pre-shift and post-shift time."

Ed's eyes tracked down the pages, but Mack knew it was all for show.

"It's not in here," he finally said.

"How long have you worked for Polson Reed?"

"Twenty years."

"When did you first start doing the route pay?"

Ed's face lost some of its surety. "I suppose it was about five years ago. The union negotiated it all. That route pay was hotly debated."

"Oh," said Mack. "And how did you come to your understanding of what the route pay is for?"

"Sorry?" Ed's brow furrowed.

"If it wasn't written down in any official documents, how did you know the route pay was separate compensation for pre- and post-shift time?"

"I don't—" Ed hesitated. Mack smiled pleasantly at him. Was it his imagination or was Ed's sculpted hair looking a little out of place? "I can't recall. That was some time ago."

"Did you sit in on any meetings with the union rep?" Mack asked.

"No," said Ed.

"Were there any emails or phone calls about it?"

"No, not that I recall."

"If it isn't in the handbook, how do you communicate to the drivers what this route pay is for?" Mack asked, sliding a pen through his fingers. He was fully prepared for Ed to try to lie Polson Reed out of this mess, but that's what preparation was for.

Ed's pause was long enough to suggest suspicion. "We tell them about it in their onboarding process."

"Mr. Schmidt, I've gone through all of the onboarding materials. There's nothing in there about pre- and post-shift route pay," Mack said evenly.

"Sure, but we tell them about it," Ed insisted. "Verbally."

"So this route pay then, there's nothing you do to show it is separate compensation for pre-shift and post-shift work. You have a formula by which you calculated it, but that formula isn't written down anywhere. Is that right, Mr. Schmidt?" Mack asked.

Ed glanced at his lawyer and then back to Mack when Meghan offered no indications of what to do. "Yeah, but we tell them about it," he insisted.

"Okay then. Thank you for your time today," Mack said.

*

With no evidence backing up his claims, Ed's testimony about the route pay's purpose was on thin ice, but not quite thin enough. Next up was the union rep, who Mack fervently hoped would have evidence to prove Ed a liar. The day before his meeting with the union rep, he got a phone call from Patrick, one of the drivers. With hardly a greeting, Patrick said, "Mr. Poyfair, I heard that one of our union reps went out to dinner with one of Polson Reed's lawyers to review their testimony. Now, I don't know this for a fact, but that's the word going around."

Mack looked at his notes for the following day's deposition and sighed. "Thanks for letting me know, Patrick." They said their good-byes and hung up. Those damn Polson Reed lawyers were going to influence every deposition he took. In the end, would he able to trust any information he got from the union rep? Mack pulled his notes over from the corner of his desk and started modifying them. If they were going to try to shade the evidence, then the least Mack could do is make them look shady.

An hour later, he was off to a meeting with Aubrey Vassos at her office at the university to go over the case and the penalties he was seeking. While some might have done this over email, Mack wanted no written record of this conversation as there would be some back and forth about how PAGA could be applied.

Despite its small size, Aubrey's office had a cozy rather than cluttered feel. Her desk photos mostly featured her with a border collie, and her stacks of papers were all neatly organized into trays and clipped together with the edges lined up. She had a clear central space on her desk where the two of them could pass materials without disturbing any knickknacks.

Aubrey settled into her desk chair after greeting him and pushed some dark curls back from her face. "Shall we begin?" she asked. Her voice was cheerful and smooth.

"Absolutely," said Mack. "As I mentioned in the interview, we're working on a case against Polson Reed Trucking. We're planning to take an unusual angle on it if our initial class action falls through. Have you heard of the Private Attorneys General Act?"

"I have not," she said.

Mack wasn't surprised; it was still relatively new in the legal world and hadn't been used extensively. "Basically, PAGA provides for penalties on behalf of the state of California. Three-quarters of the penalties will go to the Labor and Workforce Development Agency, and one-quarter goes to the employees. My firm can claim all the attorney fees and costs if we're successful. The penalty is applied for every instance of the infraction for every employee."

Aubrey nodded.

"There are over six hundred drivers involved in this, and they have various times of employment with Polson Reed over the liability period. You can see how this is getting complicated."

"That is a fair amount of numbers to crunch." Aubrey smiled.

"We're going to need a report that details the number of instances, as well as the penalties applicable. One hundred dollars for the first violation and two hundred for every violation following. Each pay period during the year preceding the filing of the complaint must be computed separately and very carefully. I need to be able to argue for maximum penalties. If there is one mistake, everything will be discredited. Polson Reed's lawyers will likely want to depose you after we list you as our expert. I forget now, did you say you had been through a deposition before?"

"I have been through a few," she said.

Her poised manner left him little doubt that she would handle it fine, but it was still crucial that she be prepared for the sorts of questions they would ask. Having sat through a few of them with Harry Clark at the helm, Mack knew what to tell her. "I think you'll manage fairly well, but I do want to coach you on a few things."

Her expression remained open. This was what had made Mack willing to pay her hefty retainer. She listened and absorbed without assuming she knew better.

"Depositions aren't an attempt to get at the truth," he said. "They're always setting up an argument and trying to put words in your mouth. You've got to be careful about what you say. They're not just going to ask about the mathematics and what formulas you used and all of that. They're going to question whether I pressured you on certain numbers. They'll ask you questions outside your expertise so that they can argue later that you agreed with them. I need you to stick to what you know and the numbers you come up with. As our expert, you should avoid agreeing with them as much as possible. They'll twist it."

Her placid expression didn't shift an inch. "I understand. You've hired me to support your case and objectively calculate the numbers."

"Yes," Mack said.

"It should not be a problem, Mr. Poyfair," she said. "Now, do you have the materials I'll need?"

Mack opened his briefcase and passed over a folder full of documents. There were copies of employment records for each driver, as well as information on

PAGA and the applicable penalties. "If you need anything else, just let me know."

"We're looking at time pre-shifts and post-shifts, yes?" Aubrey asked, accepting the folder and opening it to skim a few pages.

"Yes," Mack confirmed. "Time they are working before they are actually being paid. Each shift has pre-shift and post-shift work that isn't accounted for in the drivers' paychecks, along with unloading time, refueling, making minor repairs, and filling out paperwork. I also would like you to account for meal and rest breaks in part of the final report. Right now those are off the table, but we're working on getting a reversal of that."

"Okay. I'll get to work on this. I'll have a figure for you in a couple weeks, along with a full report." She stood and Mack followed her lead. They shook hands and parted.

Chapter 7

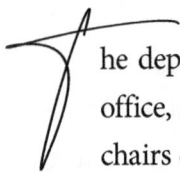

he deposition of the union rep was to be in her office, a small, dark space with a desk and some chairs crammed into it. Sally Ames looked like a woman who had earned her retirement years, but she wasn't there just yet with two years to go. Her desk held photos of people Mack presumed were her children and grandchildren, but these frames were all pushed askew by paperwork and binders littering the scarred wooden desk that had likely been through several union reps in its lifetime. *No retirement for the furniture*, Mack thought.

After a long, irritating drive through morning traffic, Mack was eager to get the deposition going.

"It's good to meet you, Ms. Ames," Mack said.

She nodded. "Let's get to it, Mr. Poyfair," she said.

He smiled warmly at her. "This is Harry Clark," Mack said, gesturing to the opposing lawyer who was wearing a gray suit that made his eyes look positively icy. The pressed-lip smile he gave Mack at this introduction didn't help the impression.

"I'm familiar with Mr. Clark," Sally said tersely.

"Of course you are," Mack said. "You two went out to dinner the other night, didn't you?"

"Yes," Sally said.

"Did you talk about the case?" Mack asked.

"I don't remember any specifics," she said, leaning back in her wheeled computer chair.

"You can't remember? It was only a couple of days ago," Mack said.

"I remember in general," she said defensively. "We did chat about it."

"Did route pay come up?"

"I don't remember the specifics," she insisted.

"Okay," Mack conceded. "Let's talk about the union negotiations. About five years ago you were involved in these negotiations, correct?"

"There's always a whole pack of us when it comes to those things."

"Who all was on your side in those negotiations? Tell me everyone you can remember."

Mack noted down every name Sally mentioned. The list was up to ten people when she said, "That's everyone, I think."

"At these negotiations," Mack said, "you all try to come to a collective decision on things, correct?"

"Yes. That's why they're negotiations and not dictations," Sally said. "The ultimate result is a collective bargaining agreement."

"And that's a document of everything important agreed upon?" Mack asked. "It's written out?"

"Yes."

"So when you were in these negotiations five years ago, did you talk about the route pay and what it was for?"

"I don't recall. There were several meetings. It took days." Sally reached out to move a photo frame a little closer to safety, away from the edge of her desk.

"The definition of route pay wasn't in the collective bargaining agreement, or CBA as it is often referred to," Mack said.

Sally shrugged. "I don't recall us having any discussions about it."

"Ed Schmidt said the topic of route pay was 'hotly debated,'" Mack said.

"I don't remember any debates about it, hot or otherwise. I don't remember discussing what the route pay was for. Then again, I wasn't there for every second of every meeting. I could have been out for one of the days and maybe that's when this 'hot debate' took place."

"I see. So what is the route pay for?" Mack asked.

"I have no idea," Sally said.

Mack wasn't sure he believed that she had no idea at all, but it was an answer worth taking.

"Ed said there was a study undertaken to determine the time of pre-shift and post-shift work to figure out the route pay. Have you ever seen a study on that?"

"No," she answered.

"How did you all come up with the route pay? The amount, I mean," Mack asked.

"I have no idea."

*

Over the next few days, Mack talked with various other union workers and supervisors, asking them if they knew what the route pay was for and how it was calculated. The answers were always some variation of not knowing.

Mack, Gloria, and Antonia had just reviewed the depositions completed so far and were clustered around the small wooden table serving as their break area. "I think it's safe to say they retroactively decided the route pay was for pre-shift and post-shift time just to try to get out of this case," Mack said. "The problem is we have no evidence to support that."

"It's one side's word against the other," said Antonia. "That's not the worst situation to be in. They have no evidence supporting their statement either."

"Except *we* need to prove they've done something wrong here, and the judge is Keats," said Gloria, a dour expression on her face. "He's going to side with the employer. They're going to say it was for the pre-shift and post-shift work. If we have no evidence to refute that claim, Keats is going to back them, and the case will be over." She tapped the eraser end of her pencil on the legal pad in front of her.

"Let's not get ahead of ourselves," Mack said, preferring Antonia's more optimistic viewpoint but knowing Gloria was right. They needed to keep looking for evidence to prove Polson Reed was lying about the route pay. Without that, every bit of work on the case was lost time, and every dime spent was down the drain, including the pay for their expert. Their whole case was riding on the fact that pre-shift and post-shift pay were not compensated. Having put so much into the case already, Mack wasn't ready to give up. "We need to keep looking. See if there are any records of what this route pay is for in writing.

Contact the drivers and see if they ever got any kind of notice explaining route pay."

*

This weekend the kids were with Melissa, so Mack was meeting up with some old bandmates. Mack hadn't planned on being a lawyer. He had played lead guitar in a band and attended the Musicians Institute Hollywood. But by the time he and Melissa had gotten together, he had shifted career paths to the much more stable law.

Mack met up with Frank, Ryan, Jack, and Janna at Spoons Grill and Bar. When Melissa first met his former bandmates, Mack had seen the passage of time in sharp relief. Without her, he felt it more. What was left of who he had been before? After meeting Melissa, Mack had continued to play the guitar for a time, but it had been relegated to a hobby, and then soon it was something only used for playing lullabies. When he became fully embroiled in his old law firm, the guitar playing had slipped away entirely. These friends had known him through such a variety of times in his life; it was easy for them to see him as still him, but when Mack thought about his life in snapshots, no one would suspect Mack the guitar player was Mack the husband or Mack the divorced, independent lawyer. They all felt like different people.

"How are things going with the new firm?" Jack asked over their first round.

"We're trucking along," Mack said. "Ha. Accidental pun," he realized. "Most of our attention is on a trucking company case at the moment."

"More people you're rescuing from being criminally underpaid?" Janna had always teased him about going into law so he could play the hero for people. He did like being someone's hero, but he hadn't particularly felt like a hero since before he and Melissa had split. He had stopped being her hero and she had stopped needing one.

"Wouldn't you want to get compensated for time you gave to your job?" asked Mack.

"Are you suggesting they aren't being paid at all?" Janna asked, raising one eyebrow.

"No. Just that they aren't being paid for *all* of the work they're doing."

"Well, good for you," said Frank. "I don't think I'd have the guts to leave the safety of having partners and run my own business as my sole source of income."

"Julia would never let you run your own business," Ryan said. "You'd be in the hole in a week."

Mack chose not to share the fact that technically, his business was now in the hole or that he'd just dipped into his line of credit to pay the twenty-thousand-dollar retainer for Aubrey Vassos. Gloria was right though; Aubrey was the perfect person for the job.

"I've sort of got my own business, too," Frank said. "The band is my business."

"You do none of the money management for Porsche," Jack pointed out. "That's all me."

Jack and Frank were still in a cover band called Porsche that mostly did weddings. In fact, Porsche had played at Mack and Melissa's wedding.

"Yeah, but they call me to book the gigs," Frank said. "And besides, you're an accountant for a living. Why wouldn't you manage the band's money?"

"People call whoever they know in the band," argued Jack.

"We should all get together sometime with our instruments," said Ryan. "See if we can still stay together on a single Rolling Stones song."

"We know Frank and I can still do it," said Jack. "Did you guys all forget how to play?"

Janna and Ryan protested that their respective keyboard and bass guitar skills were still perfectly intact. "Plus," added Janna, "my vocals would now outshine our former lead singer." She nodded at Mack. "I sing to my daughter on a daily basis, plus I'm doing vocal coaching now."

Mack hesitated to defend his own proficiency. It had been nearly eight years since he had touched a guitar, and his desire to sing had died off amid the separation and divorce.

*

Thoughts about guitar playing lingered in his mind over the weekend, and when Mack picked up the kids on Sunday night, he asked Melissa about his acoustic guitar. He had sold his electric one when he and Melissa had Ava, but he had never been willing to let go of the acoustic one, even after he'd stopped playing.

"I think it's here somewhere because I don't remember unpacking it at the new house," he said.

Melissa crossed her arms and leaned against the wall of the entryway. "If it's here, it must be in the attic. That's where I stashed everything that was getting in the way and wasn't being used."

The kids were still scrambling around the house to collect their things, so Mack asked, "Can I take a look?"

"Sure. You know where it is." She went into the kitchen and Mack headed straight up the stairs and climbed the ladder leading into the attic space.

Despite annual spring cleanings and purges throughout their years of marriage, the attic was still packed with memorabilia, old furniture, and retired exercise equipment. Mack figured the guitar would be hanging out in a corner, protected inside its black case with a photograph of the old band taped to the outside. The lighting for this space was weak and it took time for Mack's eyes to adjust. Once they did, he started hunting, checking the nooks and crannies created by dressers and tabletops leaning on walls. Melissa liked refurbishing furniture she found at yard sales, but most of those projects took years for her to complete. As a result, there was no shortage of hulking, scratched furniture taking up attic space. A bookcase was pressed to one side of the room, with the angled roof forming a triangular hiding space behind it. It was there that Mack found his guitar case. Next to it, there was a box labelled "Band Stuff." He opened it up and found rehearsal music for his old band as well as extra strings, picks, and recordings they had made themselves. He closed it back up and started to nudge it toward the opening in the floor.

Mack's eyes drifted to a plastic tote labelled "M&M." It was in the farthest corner of the attic from the trapdoor, and that was by design. When Mack moved out, there had been an uncomfortable conversation about what to do with certain things, like their wedding album. Neither of them claimed to want it, but throwing it out seemed wrong. The kids might be interested one day and it was a part of their lives, even if it was over. In the end, they had taken a tote and labelled it with their initials. Anything that marked their time together went into the tote. Even as Mack looked away from it, the image of Melissa on their wedding day opened in his mind. It was easy to be happy when there were so few needs to be met.

*

That night after the kids were asleep, Mack took out his guitar and went out into the dark backyard. He didn't quite know why he felt the need to try playing his guitar again. Partly a trip down memory lane and partly an attempt to reintegrate who he once was with who he was now, perhaps. Maybe it was time to let some things from the past back into his life.

The first chords were hesitant and not quite right. In the "Band Stuff" box, he hadn't found any of his guitar study books that laid out chord diagrams. He'd gotten rid of those, thinking he'd never forget the way to contort his fingers, but it turns out he had. Through trial and error, he found some familiar motions and started playing through the easiest tunes he could remember—ones he would play to Ava and Dev as babies. He played a halting "Twinkle, Twinkle Little

Star" followed by "Hush Little Baby." Then he thought he'd take a crack at an old favorite from his cover band days: Eric Clapton's "Crossroads."

After stumbling through it a few times, he put the guitar away. His fingertips had lost their callouses and the strings had bit red and white stripes into them. It took time to gain those skills he'd once had, and it had taken time to lose them. He wasn't starting from zero though.

Chapter 8

That Monday morning, Mack was greeted at the office by Isaiah, who was viciously twisting his Angels cap. "Last Friday, Amanda and Jacob were fired," he said, not waiting for Mack to make it to his desk. "You said we'd all be protected. You said they would be afraid to touch us and now those two are out of their jobs."

Mack frowned and set his briefcase on his desk. "It's illegal for them to retaliate against suing employees by firing them. What were the reasons given for the terminations?"

"Jacob scraped a side mirror and Amanda returned a truck with a dinged bumper or some shit. They never would have been fired for that crap before. Polson Reed is coming after us," said Isaiah. "Amanda and Jacob both have families to support, and who's going to be next? I talked them into this and now they have no jobs!" Isaiah collapsed into the chair across from Mack's desk and put his head in his hands. "I can't believe I did this to them. I just didn't want to lose my job and now..." He shook his head.

Tension raced through Mack. His weekend had ended on such an optimistic note and now, he could feel it all slipping away again. "Isaiah, based on what I've seen in the employment records, I agree that these minor incidents would likely have been forgiven by Polson Reed."

"So it is my fault. I started this whole lawsuit thing and now I've cost them their jobs."

"It is not your fault," Mack said, and Isaiah's head came up. "They will get their fair compensation just like you will when this is all said and done. For now, I will contact the defense counsel and have them investigate these terminations. It should be enough to stop Polson Reed from further frivolous firings."

"What about Amanda and Jacob? What are they going to do?" he asked.

"I'm afraid I can't do much about that," Mack said. "Everything will be fine in the end. You'll see."

Isaiah still looked miserable, so Mack added again, "This is not your fault. This is Polson Reed being dicks. We're going to make them pay."

Isaiah nodded halfheartedly and left.

Mack immediately drafted a letter to Harry Clark and his team suggesting they check into the recent firings of plaintiffs and sent it off. Couldn't a week ever start off easy?

*

Mack's letter had the desired effect, and things calmed down at Polson Reed for the beleaguered drivers. A month after the firing incident, the defense asked for a deposition of Aubrey Vassos. Meghan Moore flew down from Ohio to do this deposition on her own, once again at the imposing office building in LA. Today her blonde hair was curled and half up. The look was a lot softer than the severe professional she had presented at the depositions of the drivers. Mack wondered if it was intentional or if she simply felt more relaxed without the more experienced lawyer around.

The deposition got underway with Aubrey first detailing her report and how she arrived at the final number of seventeen million dollars. It soon became clear that although Meghan was not the primary associate, she was very good at her job. Mack worked hard to keep a focused and calm expression. He glanced at Aubrey and noted that she didn't seem at all bothered by the high-pressure questions. That was good, but Mack worried Meghan would catch her off-guard.

"How involved was Mr. Poyfair in arriving at your results?" Meghan asked.

"He provided me with the information I needed."

"So you didn't ask any of the drivers about their pre-shift and post-shift duties?"

"No," said Aubrey.

Mack could see where this was going.

"You trusted Mr. Poyfair's information on these duties? The amount of time they took and that they were supposedly unpaid?" Meghan asked.

"I used the employment records and paystubs he provided me to make my calculations."

"You took Mr. Poyfair's claims seriously," Meghan stated. "Did he guide you through these calculations?"

"I'm the mathematician, Ms. Moore," said Aubrey. "He provided me with raw data and the legal information I needed, but I did the calculations."

"What if that data were influenced in some way?" she pressed. "Who decided how long this pre-shift and post-shift work takes?"

"We used the estimate that a Polson Reed employee provided of an hour and a half."

"Who told you about that estimate? Did you hear it from the employee directly?"

"No. Mr. Poyfair gave me the estimate."

"This is the same estimate that was used for the route pay?" Meghan asked.

"My understanding is that the route pay isn't payment for the pre-shift and post-shift work," said Aubrey.

"Sure. And that information comes from…?" Meghan asked.

"Mr. Poyfair," said Aubrey. To her credit, she tried to refocus on her points. "I'm here only to explain how I arrived at my figures, and I believe I've done that. I calculated how many times Polson Reed did not pay each of their drivers for work time, and I calculated how much was owed in terms of penalties and wages."

"But all of those calculations were based on Mr. Poyfair's numbers and his claim that the drivers are owed payment for that time, correct?" Meghan asked.

"Yes," Aubrey conceded. "And I arrived at the conclusion that Polson Reed owes seventeen million in wages and penalties."

It was impressive to see Meghan take the reins on this deposition. In many ways, Mack wished it hadn't been against his expert, but Meghan's capability was better volleyed by Aubrey than it would have been by any one of the drivers.

"A conclusion you arrived at without speaking to any of the drivers. A conclusion arrived at by relying on Mr. Poyfair, the lawyer for the drivers, to provide the account of what these drivers did."

It wasn't a question, but Aubrey answered anyway with a simple, "Yes."

"How much do you know about the compensation practices in the trucking industry, Ms. Vassos?"

Aubrey shifted slightly in her chair. "I have learned a lot about it in my preparation of the report."

"Have you ever prepared a report like this before?"

She squared her shoulders. "No."

"The trucking industry is significantly more complicated than many other industries. They have special rules and are a unique corner of the job market. With no prior expertise in this area, what makes you qualified to offer an opinion on this case?" Meghan asked.

"I have a PhD in mathematics. I am more than qualified to make calculations based on numbers gleaned from evidence provided."

"But again, how was that evidence provided to you?"

"Mr. Poyfair."

"And you have no personal experience in or expertise on the trucking industry prior to the information provided by Mr. Poyfair?"

"No," Aubrey admitted.

They wrapped it up soon after and Mack bid Aubrey a farewell outside the office building. Meghan exited the building herself and Mack called to her before she could make for the parking garage.

"Ms. Moore!" he said.

She turned and waited as he approached.

"You did incredibly well in there," he said.

"Thank you," she said. "That's very sportsman-like of you to say."

Mack smiled and a sudden impulse seized him. "Do you want to grab a drink?"

She tilted her head and appeared to be taking the measure of his intentions. "All right," she said. "Let's grab a drink."

They walked across the street to a dark bar and settled at a high-top table with leather seats. Meghan ordered a gin and tonic while Mack had a beer.

"So what do you do for fun in Ohio?" he asked.

"Oh, football games and a lot of drinking," she said lightly.

"Football?"

"I *love* football," she said with a seriousness more befitting a Texan than an Ohioan.

"I'm a big fan of the sport myself, though I grew up a Cowboys fan and I'm sure you disagree."

"Absolutely!"

Mack was tickled at her enthusiasm and the two chatted football for a while. As the second round arrived the topics of conversation drifted on.

"This is the closest thing I've had to a vacation in... I don't know, five years?" she said. "California is nice, and I plan to sneak in a beach session before I have to fly back to Ohio."

"I've been here for about twenty years now," Mack said. "I grew up in Texas, of course, but I came out here when I was twenty-one to attend the Musicians Institute."

Her eyebrows rose and she leaned across the small table to place a hand over his. "You're a musician? Tell the truth, is being a lawyer your side hustle?" Her eyes sparkled with humor, and Mack chuckled.

Her hand on his gave him pause, but he didn't move it as he replied, "That would have been the idea back then. It's probably more accurate to say I *was* a musician."

"You don't play anymore?"

"Lately, I have been picking up my old guitar again."

"I've had just enough gin to confess that I have a weakness for musicians," she said, sliding her hand slightly up his arm.

"Clever, capable women are my undoing," Mack said, leaning further forward until they kissed.

She smiled and the two paid their tabs and left the bar, but out on the sidewalk, their practical legal minds resurfaced simultaneously.

"You know," she said, "it was lovely to talk with you, but…"

"We're up against each other in a huge case," Mack finished.

"It doesn't seem like the best career move for me," she said.

"Especially not after that killer deposition," Mack agreed.

She extended her hand and Mack grasped it for a firm shake. She gripped a little harder than necessary as if to affirm the professionalism of their little drinks meeting. "It was a pleasure to work against you today, Mr. Poyfair."

"It was a pleasure to see you work, Ms. Moore," he returned. Then they parted ways—her to her LA hotel and him to his empty home in Orange County.

*

It had been some time since their initial appeal to the Ninth Circuit regarding the meal breaks and rest breaks, but that was typical of the Ninth Circuit.

Briefs had been flowing back and forth regarding the issue throughout the depositions and preparations for the PAGA case. Finally, a hearing was called in which the matter was discussed. Another long silence followed while Mack, Antonia, and Gloria worked to uncover as much as they could against the claim that route pay covered pre- and post-shift work time. This route pay issue could completely undo the only case that was currently actionable against Polson Reed, and the stress was starting to show in Mack's appearance.

As he ran his hand through his hair in frustration once more, hairs sprinkled onto his desk. He didn't have a genetic predisposition to hair loss and the shower of dark strands was unnerving. He brushed the hairs away into the trash bin under his desk and went back to perusing the employment documents, searching for any overt statements regarding the route pay. Tempted as he was to keep raking his hand through his hair, he settled for clicking a pen instead. He needed to change that habit before he went bald.

After another unsuccessful hunt through the driver compensation documents, Mack checked his messages and mail. There was something from the Ninth Circuit waiting. Tensely, he opened it and read the decision. He smacked his pen down on the desk and stood, startling Antonia.

"Is everything all right?" she asked.

"It's fantastic. We got the reversal."

Gloria looked up from her work now too. "What?"

"The Ninth Circuit reversed the F Quad-A preemption of the breaks."

Gloria raised her arms in silent triumph.

"We've got to get started on the class action for the breaks," Mack said. "Let's set up together at the breakroom table and get started. I want to hit them with both suits at the same time as much as possible."

Polson Reed's concern would increase from twelve drivers to six hundred and sixty-five if their class certification was approved. Mack, Antonia, and Gloria gathered around their break table, which at this point was doubling as a conference room for team meetings. Gloria and Antonia had never been through the class certification process before, and Mack felt the pressure to be the wise leader.

"What we have to do here is prove that these twelve representatives are good examples of an entire class, and we need to prove that we are can litigate a class action," Mack said. "We've got to prepare the motion for class certification on the meal breaks and rest breaks, so it's time to gather everything together. We need the depositions ready for presentation on that too, as well as the PAGA case."

Gloria made a note. "I'll get started on the class certification. What's the plan going forward with the pre- and post-shift work? That route pay claim is still holding."

"To discredit Schmidt's testimony about the route pay, we're going to use their paperwork against them. We have the collective bargaining agreement from the union meeting that settled the route pay. This has no mention of the route pay's purpose or calculation. Plus, we have all their on-boarding materials and their employee handbook. None of which mention paying the drivers for pre-shift or post-shift time." Mack pushed the piles of papers forward to the center of the table. "We need to connect the dots between the testimony, our claims, and the documents to show how they prove our claims. We need to make the judge doubt Schmidt's route pay statement.

"And it's time to get all the drivers together again." At this point, it had been a few months since they'd all gathered to discuss the status of the case. Although Mack kept in regular touch with many of them, it was time for a large-scale update and to see if they had anything more to offer that might add to the support of the certification request or debunk Schmidt's route pay assertions.

*

Over the next few days, Antonia tirelessly coordinated the odd schedules of the truckers and within two weeks, another meeting was taking place in the Holiday Inn Express conference room in the late evening—the only time all twelve plaintiffs were available. Mack had a tight rein on his nerves. The class certification was crucial to the future of the case, and he wanted everyone in the room to believe it was going to happen, including himself.

"As we informed you all last week, we got the reversal on the meal breaks and rest breaks. So we are moving for class certification on that right now," Mack told the gathered drivers. "We're also still pursuing compensation for your pre-shift and post-shift work using the Private Attorneys General Act," Mack said. "The first means that they will owe penalties for every instance where you were not paid for your time. This approach is somewhat unconventional, but it will put Polson Reed in their place and force a policy change on top of the penalties.

"Since we didn't have the rest breaks and meal breaks on the table before, we weren't actually pursuing a class-action lawsuit. Given that the situation has changed to include that, I think it's important that you understand the certification process."

He explained the process and eyes glazed over around the room.

"It's this simple: You weren't paid for all our time and now we've got to show that to the judge. And show that this is a problem throughout the company. All those depositions you guys did and all the other ones we did with the Polson Reed supervisors and union folk, we're bringing it all together for this side of the case too," Mack said. "We're going to hit some highlights tonight and we want to hear anything you've got to strengthen either or both of our two separate actions."

In an effort to keep their attention, he changed it up by playing the bit of Ed Schmidt's deposition where he claimed route pay was for the pre-shift and post-shift work. The video clip had a few drivers shaking their heads and others rolling their eyes. One said, "What a phony corporate asshole he's turned into."

Mack privately agreed.

After presenting the facts they'd gathered regarding the route pay claim, Mack said, "I'm going to tell it to you straight. Right now, we need something to prove that route pay is *not* for pre-shift and post-shift work in order for our PAGA lawsuit to have a good shot. I know Antonia got in touch with all of you about this, so if you've come up with anything, we need to hear it. Let's take a quick break before we get into any more of this."

As Mack topped up his cup of coffee, Barry approached him. "Mr. Poyfair?" he said. "Antonia had called me about that route pay stuff and I was thinking about it. I dug through some old memos." The young man smiled ruefully. "My mom calls me a packrat, but my dad always told me to keep records of everything work-related. Anyway"— he reached into his pocket and pulled out a crumpled piece of paper—"it doesn't say route pay on it, but I think it might be helpful."

Mack set down his coffee cup to smooth out the page and read it. The typed words sent his confidence in the case soaring.

Chapter 9

"Barry," Mack said, "This is *exactly* what we needed." He called Gloria over and handed her the paper.

"What's this?" she asked after reading it.

"Barry had it."

"How did he get it?"

Mack looked at Barry to explain.

"We were at a driver meeting. I suppose it was about three years ago."

Mack looked down at the memo again and checked the date on it. Three years ago.

"Somehow the whole unpaid work topic came up. The supervisor at the meeting said it was all part of our jobs and the thirty-two cents a mile covered it, like it was only that high because of the extra work," Barry said. "They told us we're professional drivers so it's on us to get the job done and if we couldn't get it done in enough time to make a reasonable wage that was our own fault. I remember he said, 'We don't know what you're up to on the road.' Like they were accusing us of padding our mileage or something. So anyway, a couple days after that meeting this memo is sent out." He pointed to the paper in Gloria's hands.

Mack read it again: *You get paid very well. I don't want to hear that you can't get your pre-shift and post-shift work done without extra money. There is no separate compensation for pre-shift and post-shift work. That's all part of the job.*

At the top was a Polson Reed letterhead and the date of the memo. At the bottom was the supervisor's signature.

"Barry, tell your mother that packrats are the saving grace for many a problem in the world," Mack said, grinning.

*

Later that week, Mack submitted Barry's evidence along with everything else for the PAGA case. They were still preparing the class certification request, so Mack found himself easily distracted during the wait for the trial date of the PAGA case.

It was only thrust to the forefront again when the defendants' request for summary judgment came through.

"What the hell is this," Mack said, staring at the document. Gloria had brought it to his attention after she had spotted the update on the court portal.

"They want summary judgment based on what Ed Schmidt said about the route pay. They're saying there's obviously no case given that the supposed unpaid time is paid," Gloria said.

"Thanks," Mack snapped. "As if I couldn't understand that myself."

"Hey." She popped a hand on her hip and stared at him. "Don't shoot the messenger."

Mack waved a hand at her. "Sorry, sorry. I know." He shoved a hand through his hair, realized what he was doing and shook out the hand.

Antonia approached then and placed a homemade brownie on a plate next to Mack's desk phone. "Judge Keats has to be able to see from our briefs that there's nothing backing up that route pay nonsense. Barry's note says just the opposite."

Mack stared at the brownie for a second. Antonia had taken to bringing in treats on Fridays and her popping over with one plated up like this meant she had felt his tension across the room.

Although Poyfair Law had no statements in their documentation about what the route pay was for, that didn't constitute evidence that it wasn't for the pre-shift and post-shift work. Barry's note was the best they had, but the employee who wrote it hadn't worked for Polson Reed for well over three years now. It didn't address the route pay directly, either. Mack caught his own hand reaching for his hair again and diverted it to the brownie instead. Two bites and it was gone.

"There's not much we can do about it now," he grumbled.

"We're better off putting our energy into the class action for now," said Gloria. "I'm sure we'll know soon enough whether that summary judgment comes through in their favor."

Her tone said it all. Mack knew it as well as she did: Keats was a conservative judge who frequently landed on the side of big business. Monroe Casper had played their cards exactly right and that really pissed off Mack.

*

It was Dev's birthday on Saturday and Melissa had put together a birthday party for him. Mack was invited along with the parents of all Dev's friends, including Gloria whose son Liam went to the same school as Dev. Mack had been relieved when Gloria mentioned she was going to the party. Mack knew a few of Dev's friends' parents, but the divorce had made the still-together parent sets less willing to talk to Mack. He didn't know if the same was true for Melissa, but he suspected it was. It seemed like sometimes people thought divorce could be caught like the flu so they never wanted to stand too close. It wasn't true of close friends, but acquaintances like his kids' friends' parents...they didn't know Mack or Melissa well enough to stay personally involved.

Mack arrived early for the party to offer his assistance. An early fall cookout was an easy way to feed a slew of people, but it did take some management of the grill and kitchen at the same time, and Melissa never liked much interference in her kitchen. Ava answered the door when he arrived. He followed her to the kitchen where Melissa was performing some kind of choreographed cooking dance that Mack had seen before at holidays, celebrations, and neighborhood gatherings. Melissa could prepare a feast blindfolded in that kitchen.

She paused midway through a turn from the refrigerator to the center island when she caught sight of Mack. "Oh," she said. "You're here early."

"I wanted to say happy birthday to Dev before anyone else got here. Thought I'd offer to help too. Maybe get the grill going for you?"

Melissa glanced to the door that led out of the kitchen to the fenced in backyard. "Um…"

"Shonda's dad is already starting it," said Ava, taking her place by the sink to wash vegetables.

Mack's eyes flicked to the door, and he shrugged. "Maybe Martin could use a hand. The propane is a little finicky."

"Sure," said Melissa. "Dev's out there too, playing with Shonda. Can I talk to you for a second first?"

"Yeah." Mack could already tell what was on Melissa's mind. It was obvious in her hesitation to say Martin was there, and in her startled face at his early appearance. Still, he followed her into the laundry room next to the back door.

"I didn't expect you early. It would be nice to have a heads-up," she said.

"Right, sorry. Just figured twenty minutes wouldn't be a big deal and it is Dev's birthday."

"It's fine. Just, a heads-up would be good. Also…" She took a deep breath. "A heads-up for you. Martin and I have gone on a couple dates."

"I figured it was something like that," Mack said. "You weren't planning on telling me that today, huh?"

"I didn't think the two of you would be alone together for any real length of time and it isn't anything significant yet. I haven't said anything to the kids and I'd rather we didn't unless it becomes something more than a couple dates." Her earnest brown eyes always turned Mack sympathetic.

"Got it," he said, smiling reassuringly. "No worries. We'll keep the talk to burgers."

Melissa's lips curled up a bit. "Thank you."

They left the closeted room and Melissa went back to her dance while Mack stepped out the door.

He gave Martin a nod of greeting and went to where Dev was dribbling a basketball near the hoop in the back corner of the yard. He was facing off against Shonda.

"Happy birthday, kiddo!" Mack said, hoping for a hug but not certain Dev would be willing to give one in the presence of a friend.

Dev abandoned the ball to come over to his father. "I don't have to help with the party because it's my birthday," he said.

"Makes sense," Mack said. "I got a present here for you if you want."

"Mom said I get to open presents later," Dev said, his eyes fixed on the red papered box despite this statement.

"I think she'd make an exception for the gift from Dad," he said.

That was all the encouragement Dev needed to pluck it from his father's hands and sit down on the ground to tear it open.

"Awesome!" He took out the Nintendo 3DS and Shonda came over to check it out. "And it's blue!"

"Yep. There's some games in there too."

"Thanks Dad!"

"Happy birthday, bud. One thing though, you probably want to put that away in your room before all your guests arrive. Your mom won't like it if someone's got their face glued to a screen all day."

"Okay."

Mack didn't know if the warning would stick because Dev's eyes were already locked on the screen and Shonda was right next to him. Mack was forgotten so he went over to the grill where Martin was putting the first burger patties on.

"How's it going there, Martin?"

"Pretty good."

They made awkward chat for a few minutes about work and weather and then Ava came outside bearing some bowls to place on the long folding table meant to serve as a buffet. Mack followed her when she went back into the house and made himself busy carrying out the various foodstuffs.

It was strange to see another man at the grill in this backyard. He had let go of Melissa, during their separation and divorce, but he hadn't expected this part, where his role in this family might be filled in places, or he might be forced to share it with someone. He wasn't totally comfortable with it. If he wasn't supposed to grill on the rare occasions he and Melissa were together at this house with the kids, then what was he supposed to do?

People started arriving soon after the food was in place and the kids formed teams for a soccer game. Mack stood with Gloria and watched them play, while they tried to talk about anything but work. It proved to be rather difficult. Martin remained in charge of the grill until everyone was fed. There was cake and presents and then people started heading home. Mack didn't leave yet, nor did Martin.

"You don't have to help clean up," Melissa said while Mack shoved paper plates with half-eaten cake on them into a trash bag.

"Dev's our son," he said. "When it comes to the kids, I want you to expect my help."

Melissa pressed her lips together for a second and then went back into the house where she was washing up dishes.

After the clean-up was done and Martin left with his daughter, Mack played a quick game of checkers against Ava while Dev was absorbed in his new 3DS. Melissa sat on the couch reading *The New Yorker* with her feet up, something she always did after a party. He felt like he had a place again and then the game of checkers ended and Mack left for his home, miles away and alone.

*

After spending the remainder of the weekend puttering around his house, Mack went back to the office on Monday in a sour mood. The class certification preparation was going rather smoothly, however, so by mid-week his mood had turned around. It helped that a couple smaller cases came through the door as well. They were a small firm, so any cases they took on had to be small while the Polson Reed drivers' cases were in action. It was reassuring though to have the small trickle in addition to the rapids.

On Thursday, Mack was downright cheerful up until Judge Keats's ruling came through. The summary judgment was granted. There would be no trial for the pre- and post-shift work, which meant there would be no money from it.

"Damn!"

"Summary judgment?" asked Gloria.

"Yes."

She shook her head just a little. "Mack, I think we both knew it was likely to come out this way."

"Doesn't mean I can't be pissed that it did," he argued.

She shrugged. "I suppose you're right. Should I prepare a message for the drivers?"

"Yeah, tell them how we failed and then somehow convince them that the class action will still go through fine."

Gloria flicked her eyebrows up and then turned her attention back to her computer. "I think I'll word it a little differently," she said.

Chapter 10

*P*oyfair Law Firm was fully prepared to file a motion for class certification and Mack was eager to see this case move forward after the setback of the summary judgment. Mack, Gloria, and Antonia put all the evidence together, along with Aubrey's report and transcripts of the depositions, and created the brief. The five-hundred pages of material was sent out and after nearly a month, the opposition's reply came with almost double the pages. It was pretty much as Mack had expected. The lawyers at Monroe Casper were all from top law schools and it showed in their briefs. Mack gave Gloria a copy and they both got to reading and rereading. They only had so much time to tender their response before the hearing with Judge Keats, and the material was incredibly dense. Mack had many years of experience reading legal briefs, but this team really had a way with words. They made the simplest precepts sound incredibly complicated, and they made the absurd seem plausible.

When Gloria and Mack got together to discuss the brief two weeks after receiving the massive stack, Gloria said, "Look, I'm on our side, Mack, obviously, but this brief... It is damn convincing. They sound so reasonable. I half believe they're the ones getting screwed over."

"They sure make it sound that way." Mack raised a hand to his hair and then stopped himself. "I know this is tough reading and they are good, but this is what we do. We need to untangle their carefully woven tapestry and point the judge back at the objective."

"Did you see their claims against our fitness to handle the class action?" Gloria asked.

"Those seem the simplest to rebut," Mack said. "Do you want to start there?"

"Let's do it," she said, clicking a pen into action.

First, Monroe Casper said Poyfair Law Firm's unorthodox approach to the case proved they were unqualified as they clearly didn't know the usual proceedings.

"Our unusual approach is exactly what qualifies us," Mack said. Gloria took notes as he spoke. "Any other firm following the usual routes would have had this case tossed out already. The fact that we got it this far using these 'unorthodox' methods means we're uniquely qualified."

"Next, we've never dealt with a wage class action of this size," Gloria said. "Absurd." Gloria made more notations. "Their last point against our viability is the suggestion of a conflict of interest with the PAGA case we had going. I admit, they had that sounding pretty legitimate."

"Take a step back from their words and think about their actual allegation," Mack said. "They're saying that our other case is a conflict of interest with this case. How are those two cases at odds with one another? Both cases are made up of clients who want money from Polson Reed. That's a convergence of interests, not a conflict. Both actions are seeking justice for unpaid wages from Polson Reed. Same goal, so no conflict."

"Okay." Gloria finished her notes regarding that section.

They worked their way through the brief's main points, building the bones of their rebuttal. They sent off a polished brief a week later, but before the certification hearing could take place, there was surprising news.

"We've got a bit of a situation of good news/bad news," Mack told his colleagues. "There's been a substitution of counsel. I think we got to them. Polson Reed is definitely starting to feel the heat."

"Who did they bring in?" Gloria asked, coming around her desk to lean against the front of it.

Mack was feeling the heat too. "That's the bad news. We thought Monroe Casper was the big guns, but it's the local team from Humbert Lewis."

Humbert Lewis was an international firm with offices on both coasts of the United States, in various parts of Europe and in Singapore.

"Ugh," Gloria said, rolling her eyes. "That guy."

While amusing to see her revert to a teenager, Mack couldn't have agreed more. Aaron Norris was an asshole. More than once, Mack had been tempted to throw him out a window.

"Some combination of the second lawsuit, our class certification request, and the way this has dragged out must have convinced them they needed local counsel," he said. "I think this is a good thing for us."

"It doesn't feel like a good thing," said Antonia, her eyes wide. "Humbert Lewis is huge, bigger than Monroe Casper."

"They felt they needed someone bigger to take us on," Mack said. "It's a compliment."

"If you say so," Gloria said. "It can't hurt that they have a local base, so Polson Reed is being billed less for flights to and from Ohio."

"We'll be facing Aaron Norris and his associate, Cassidy Perkins, at the hearing next week," Mack said.

"You better practice keeping your cool," Gloria said.

"I'm cool. I told you, I see this as a good sign."

"That's all well and fine, but Norris has a way of getting under your skin." Gloria raised one challenging eyebrow and then went back around her desk to sit.

"What do you want me to do? Take up meditation? It'll be fine," he reassured her.

Mack saw Antonia glance between him and Gloria, her poor poker face revealing nervousness.

"Trust me, Antonia," Mack said. "This is great for us."

Gloria offered a small snort but didn't take her eyes from her computer screen.

*

Mack spent the night before the hearing reviewing his notes and then playing around on his guitar. He wasn't about to take up meditation, but Gloria wasn't wrong to suggest he practice keeping his cool. Mack thought strumming for an hour or so would relax him and give him a clear mind to take on Aaron Norris. He did wake up feeling refreshed and optimistic about the day. That feeling lasted up until just before heading into the hearing, when Norris greeted Mack in the hallway.

"Good to see you, Poyfair," he said, extending a hand. "I thought maybe you'd disappeared since you split with Myer and O'Toole."

Mack shook his cold hand. He was built like a linebacker and had a graying buzz cut. Mack tried not to think about his own hair in comparison. It was holding its color, but the hairline was cutting into his confidence a little.

"Opened my own firm and here we are," Mack said. "You remember Gloria?" Gloria shook Aaron's hand as well.

"Yes, of course. You followed him on his hope-filled venture, eh?" Aaron said.

"Turns out we didn't need much hope. Polson Reed is looking to be a great payday for us," Gloria said.

"Pretty confident considering you haven't even been granted your certification yet," Aaron said.

"Then we best get to it," she replied.

Aaron gestured for them to go ahead and Mack took the offer, entering the courtroom first, followed by Aaron. Gloria came in with a few of the class representatives. After the formal opening, everyone took their seats and Judge Keats called Mack forward to begin.

"We're here today seeking class certification for Unlawful Meal Period Policy Class and Failure to Separately Pay for Rest Breaks Class under the Unfair Competition Law. Our class representatives today are Isaiah Garza, Patricia Firth, Patrick Yost, Barry Beady, and Kiran Orman," said Mack. "Polson Reed Trucking established an Activity-Based Compensation scheme for their drivers to pay drivers on four components." Mack ticked off each on his fingers as he spoke. "The number of stops completed, the number of pallets delivered, the number of miles traveled, and 'route pay,' which is a lump sum payment Polson Reed claims compensates drivers for administrative tasks before and after their shifts. There is no provision for meal and rest breaks. Per California's wage-an-hour law, Polson Reed is required to provide the drivers with meal breaks. The AB Compensation scheme failed to separately compensate my clients for the rest breaks that were taken. The representatives here today are prepared to submit declarations to that effect."

Aaron rose from his seat to offer Polson Reed's objections to the admissibility of the declarations. It was a long list: hearsay, lack of foundation, improper expert opinion…

Judge Keats listened and then said, "For a class certification motion, the Court may consider evidence inadmissible at trial. Admissibility is not at issue here."

Mack went on to detail how their class fulfilled the four requirements—numerosity, commonality, typicality, and adequacy—for class action under federal regulations, using supporting testimony from the class representatives. Aaron mounted his rebuttal, bringing up his previous claims against Poyfair Law's fitness for litigating the case, in addition to arguing that there was no class-wide issue at hand.

"Both sides have made excellent points. There's a lot to consider here." Keats's eyes landed on the briefs stacked on his desk. "Is there anything further?"

"We submit, Your Honor," Mack said.

"We submit," said Aaron.

"Okay then," Judge Keats said. "Thank you, gentlemen. I will be reviewing your motion and you will hear from me when I have decided. Have a great day."

Both sides departed and Mack was quick to stride toward the exit, doing his best to avoid another interaction with Aaron.

*

Isaiah called late that afternoon. "Did the judge grant the certification?" he asked.

"Hang on there," Mack said. "It doesn't work that fast. This is federal court. It can take months before they decide this."

"Months!"

Mack felt the same about it. Every day they spent waiting was a little more debt he'd have to hope he could recover from in the end. "It probably won't be that long, but I don't want you sitting around waiting for this. We'll let you know when we know."

Isaiah sounded miserable as he accepted this information and they hung up.

*

That weekend Jack stopped by Mack's place and the two had beers on the patio. After covering work and family, Jack said, "So listen, we have this gig at Our Place, that pub in Lake Forest? It's next month and our lead guitar is due to have her baby around then. Any chance you'd want to do it?"

"Did you not hear me?" Mack asked. "I've got a career-making case in the works right now."

"All work and no play—"

Mack waved his hand to cut Jack off. "It's not all work and no play. I just spend my play hours with my kids."

Jack looked around pointedly and then arched a brow at Mack.

"There are not enough play hours leftover to be playing band gigs until two in the morning at pubs. I'm an adult now. I need to sleep sometimes."

"The gig's on a Friday night. You could sleep in the next day."

"It's not that simple. If I have court on Friday or the kids, I can't guarantee my schedule."

"It's not that hard to figure out. Worse comes to worse, you can bring the kids with!"

Mack stared at him. "To a pub. On a Friday night. Until two in the morning."

"They close at one."

"It is so obvious you don't have kids." Mack took a sip from his bottle.

"I think you should seriously consider this." Jack's face turned serious. "I'm not saying you're no fun anymore or anything like that, but I'm genuinely concerned. After you and Melissa split, you started this new law firm. Running your own business is an easy excuse to quit having a personal life and personal interests."

"I went out with you guys a couple weeks ago," Mack said. "I had drinks with that opposing counsel woman too."

"That's basically the same as work, but good for you having a drink with someone new."

Mack shook his head.

"Look, maybe I'm just desperate to get someone to fill in for our lead guitar so she isn't so worried about it." He shrugged and leaned back in his seat. "Is this case for sure going to trial?"

"We're waiting to hear whether our certification is approved," Mack said.

"How long will that take?"

"Weeks, months." Mack shrugged. "There's no way to know."

"So you might not even be working on the case when the Our Place gig rolls around?" Jack leaned forward again, smiling.

"There's always something to be doing."

"Like I said, an excuse to have no personal life."

"The case is going to get approved and when it does, we're going to have a shit ton more work to do," said Mack.

"How about you just think about it? I saw your guitar in the living room, man." He nodded behind them toward the house. "You're coming back to the music. Seriously consider it, okay? It's only a few hours one night."

"And a few hundred practices to sound good," Mack said.

"We've still got some rhythm left."

"Find someone else."

"I'll keep looking, but I'm also still going to call you up. You need to think about setting a good example for your kids."

"By being a rock 'n' roll player on the weekends?"

"By showing them that a fulfilling life has more than work in it."

"You need to stop watching afternoon talk shows," said Mack.

Jack shrugged. "They're a part of my fulfilling life."

*

Mack was prepared to wait a long time for the judgment on the certification. He was startled when the answer arrived two weeks later, and he was able to call Isaiah with the news.

"You guys are officially certified as a class," Mack said. "And we're assigned as the law firm."

Isaiah's sigh blew through the phone line. "Now what?"

He was always asking that. It was always about the next hurtle. Mack could relate.

"Now we prepare for the trial."

Chapter 11

*"I*t's not everything we asked for," Mack cautioned Gloria and Antonia as they discussed the certification. "Obviously we won the appointment as class counsel, but we did miss out on the meal break class. Judge Keats ruled there wasn't class-wide evidence and there were many individual reasons for meal breaks being missed so there was no predominance."

"So we have no pre-shift or post-shift and no meal breaks?" Gloria summed up.

"Right, but we still have the rest break claims."

"How far will that get us?" Gloria asked, crossing her arms.

"Every driver and every break from May 2008 to present," Mack said, smiling.

Her sternness softened. "Well, that's not nothing, I guess."

Because of how Mack had defined the case, the class included every driver for Polson Reed in the last four years. Six hundred and sixty-five letters needed to go out, notifying each of these drivers of their right to opt out of the case. Amid preparing for the trial, it was too much for Antonia, Gloria, and Mack to take on, so he hired an outside administrator to take care of it. Every investment he made in the case now felt like a much safer bet. With class certification in hand, Mack was feeling much more confident, and it seemed less of his hair was falling out.

He wasn't ready to take on anything else at the moment, however, so when Jack called to follow up, Mack told him no. Besides, playing a few tunes a couple nights a week wasn't going to get him in gigging shape before next month.

"It's just not going to work out right now. That trucking case I told you about is heading to trial," Mack said.

"There's always going to be a case heading to trial, if you're any good at your job," said Jack. "Don't you miss the stage?"

Did he? Could you miss something that you hadn't noticed you'd let slip away? He remembered being on a small stage at a reception hall for a wedding. Little kids twirling away on the dance floor because the adults hadn't had enough to drink yet. Later, when they had, the raucous dancing of gangly men with neckties around their heads and the bridesmaids stomping on the dance floor like their bare feet could make a sound over the band. Colored lights spinning…

"Yeah, but I'm building a business here," Mack said.

"You could have built the band with us."

Mack went to rub a hand through his hair and then stopped. Best not to encourage any more stress on the follicles. "College was different. I wasn't building a family or a business then. I've got two kids and two employees. They're all counting on me to make this work and this case will make us a name."

Jack's tone shifted back to a lighter one. "Yeah, all right, I hear you. I hope it gives you everything you need."

"Thanks," Mack said.

*

As the days went by and no opt-out notices came in, Mack's confidence rose. The more people in the class, the more powerful their case would be. Jury selection would be crucial. Since it was a federal case, there would only be six jurors and every single one would have to vote in favor of Mack's case when it came time for the verdict. Gloria, Mack, and Antonia worked on a list of questions to filter through the potential jurors. Mack knew Norris's team would nix any jurors who were squarely in the drivers' corner—people who raged against employers, blue collar workers who felt held back by the man, etc. It was inevitable in the same way that Mack would strike any potential juror who showed strong support for management. Mack and Norris would ultimately be working toward the middle-of-the-road jurors who could be swayed one way or the other, ones without hardline opinions but who perhaps leaned one way or the other. The questions Poyfair Law were preparing aimed to uncover the heavily conservative individuals and to condition the final selections to be sympathetic to the drivers' cause.

"Do the McDonald's case test," said Gloria.

"Good idea." Mack made a note.

"What's the McDonald's test?" asked Antonia.

"It's that case where the woman sued McDonald's after being burnt by their coffee," Gloria said. "It tells you whether a potential juror is open to having their initial opinions swayed."

"Sort of measures their ability to change their mind instead of sticking to their biases in spite of any new information," Mack added.

"Try it on me," Antonia said. "I want to know if I'm open-minded."

"You are," Gloria said.

Antonia blinked a couple times and looked to Mack.

"She meant it as a compliment," he said.

Antonia glanced at Gloria once more before returning to the research in front of her.

"Mack, are you open-minded?" she asked.

He took a moment to assess himself. "I like to think I am. I know I can be persuaded by proven facts."

"Fact one," said Antonia, "my friend Rose is very smart. Fact two, she's beautiful. Fact three, I think you should go on a date with her."

Mack choked on air. "Excuse me?"

Antonia shrugged one shoulder. "I think you should go on a date with her."

"Why?"

"Your ex-wife is dating again, right?"

"How did you…?" Gloria was staring at him. "I wouldn't have asked you both to come to this firm with me if I'd known you were going to become gossip buddies."

"Information," Gloria said. "Gossip is speculation."

Mack shook his head. "We need a sense of how the jurors feel about employee/employer relationships," he said.

"About Rose..." Antonia said, pulling him back to her preferred topic. "Should I set it up?"

"No," he said. "You're not even thirty. Your friend is probably ten or more years younger than me."

"I have friends who are older than me, you know," she said. "Rose is thirty-eight, for your information. Not even five years younger than you, Mr. Dramatic."

"I'm not going on a date with your friend. We're preparing for the case that is going to make us or break us, here," he said. "We need to focus on that, so we all still have jobs."

Antonia pressed her lips together and went back to her stacks of research. Other than the one make-out session with the former opposing counsel, Mack hadn't been leaning back into the dating world at all. He wasn't particularly keen on the idea, but Melissa was dating so maybe he should too. *Irrelevant,* he thought and brought his mind to the case at hand. As well as things were going at the moment, there was an entire trial in front of them where things could go awry. What would dating matter if his law firm went under in its fledgling years? His focus needed to be on this case.

Chapter 12

Fifteen potential jurors were in the courtroom waiting for Mack and Norris to start asking questions. They had no idea what the case was about yet, so now was the time for Mack to challenge their beliefs and biases to see if they leaned his way. Gloria was there to watch the reactions of those he wasn't directly questioning. It wasn't uncommon for the person in the spotlight to be on-guard while those around them were less careful about their facial expressions and physical reactions.

"Let's say you're faced with a situation where an employer doesn't pay all the employees' wages," Mack said. "For every day you work, the last hour you work for free. Does that seem okay to you?"

Down the line of potential jurors, there were varying levels of denial from vehement 'of course not' to relaxed 'not cool.' Then the question came to juror number twelve, Mary, a retired teacher.

"When you're paid a salary," she said, "you're always indebted to the employer."

"How do you mean?" Mack asked.

"I graded papers and helped students outside my work hours. I wasn't paid for that in addition to my salary. There are some jobs where work outside of the working day is just part of the job."

Mack nodded once and Gloria made a note on her list of the jurors. Mary was on the chopping block.

Aaron asked, "Isn't it the employee's responsibility to maintain accurate time logs? For example, if one is a truck driver, shouldn't they keep accurate logs of their driving time?"

The answers were mostly neutral, but one young man wearing a college sweatshirt added, "Don't they have GPSes or something to log that for them? A paper log with pen and stuff...I mean, yeah, I'd keep my own log as part of the job, but would I trust my boss not to change it after I submitted it? No way. The only way to get a fair wage is to remember your boss is always out to screw you."

Mack suppressed a smile. The kid would never make the jury with that outspoken attitude, but the other jurors heard it and their responses gave him something to go on as well. Jury selection was high-stakes poker. He was playing every person there, swaying them to believe his position, learning their beliefs through answers and unconscious body language.

"Are you all familiar with the McDonald's coffee case?" Mack began.

Nods, along with some eye rolls.

"You all find it pretty frivolous?"

"It was coffee. Who doesn't know that coffee is hot?" The man who spoke wore a suit and seemed entirely at ease in his seat. "She saw a big company and thought she could get a piece of their pie, and boy, did she."

There was general agreement around him.

"Would it change your mind," Mack continued, "if you knew that McDonald's operation manual at the time required the temperature to be at 180 to 190 degrees? At that temperature, coffee causes third-degree burns in seconds, and there were no warnings to consumers concerning that. McDonald's had received hundreds of complaints about the too-hot coffee already. Mrs. Liebeck received third-degree burns and had to have skin grafts. Do you still think her case was frivolous?"

Some of the potential jurors seemed stunned. Their answers shifted dramatically from the initial response. One, however, held out. The man in the suit said, "She'd probably had their coffee before. She knew it was hot. People shouldn't need warnings for simple common sense: hot things will burn skin."

Mack observed as the suit's remarks hit the other jurors. Next to him, Gloria made notes. This man was obviously unswayable in his opinions, which wouldn't play well for Mack's case. That was another one down.

"If an employee does work off the clock, is it the employer's responsibility to see they are paid for it if the employee doesn't complain?"

Again, a mix of answers came from the collection of people, but no one stood out.

Questions went back and forth for a time, and Mack added one more person to his "strike" list—a business owner who said employees are always trying to screw the employer over and who gave the college sweatshirt kid a sideways glance as he said it. Norris struck everyone Mack had expected him too and both sides approved the final six: a young college woman, a retired Army veteran, a barista, a doctor, an accountant, and a garbage collector.

Judge Keats thanked the jury members for their service and dismissed the ones who were not needed.

*

That night Gloria brought Liam over to Mack's house. They were working on their opening statement while the boys played video games in the living room. Ava was in her room doing homework, having declared the kitchen too loud for her to concentrate. Mack suspected she wasn't doing much homework anymore, but she'd never given Melissa or him any reason to doubt her responsibility when it came to school.

"We need to attack their main message," Mack declared. "What is it they are using against us?"

"Based on what I've seen in the declarations on their side, it seems they are going to try to lump the rest breaks in with their route pay."

"That's a hell of a lot for that measly thirty bucks to cover," said Mack.

"We should take it down to the simple math of it all. We have Schmidt's depositions claiming the route pay covered pre-shift and post-shift. He said that it was an hour and a half of work and then he gave some by-the-hour rate they used to calculate it. If that was enough to get summary judgment on the pre-shift and post-shift work, then it has to hold up next to their rest break pay claims."

"Right, okay." Mack started drafting. "It's simple math and simple wage theft. They're getting an unfair advantage over their competition by cutting corners on paying their drivers properly."

Gloria nodded. She read over his words as he typed, making suggestions along the way. When they thought they were ready, they called the boys away from their game of *Mario Kart* and Mack went to knock on Ava's door.

"Come in," she said.

Sure enough, when he opened the door, she was sprawled across her bed reading another *Nancy Drew* novel.

"Can Gloria and I borrow you for a second?" he asked. "I want to try out our opening argument on you guys."

She closed her book and popped up from the bed. While he could often see hints of the teenager to come, he could still see his little girl in this instance. Eager to be a part of her dad's work and to have her opinions heard.

She followed him to the kitchen and took a seat next to the boys. They were all lined up on one side of the table and Gloria sat at one end. Mack stood with notes in hand.

"Can I borrow some of your paper?" Ava asked Gloria. "And a pen?"

Gloria handed over a sheet of yellow legal pad paper and a pen. The boys copied Ava's request immediately. Mack and Gloria both refrained from laughing at the way each child prepared to take notes and sat up straighter. The children displayed seriousness befitting committing someone to prison.

"Ladies and gentlemen of the jury," Mack began, "Polson Reed Trucking has made repeated, unequivocal statements in the course of this case."

A couple sentences in and Ava wrote something down. The boys, seeing this, each scribbled as well. From where he stood, he could tell the boys' notes were much less pertinent. Still, he carried on. When he finished, Ava went through her notes point by point.

"No one will believe the managers are bad guys unless someone says how mean they were," Ava said. "You should have some of the drivers talk about how mad the managers got if they asked for time off or were late. Make sure the jury knows who the bad guy is."

Gloria wrote down some of her more valuable insights. Dev wanted to go next, and his notes were mainly on the theme of not knowing what certain words meant. Liam suggested the clients wear "outside clothes."

"You know, their jeans with holes and stuff. That way the jury will feel bad for them and give them lots of money."

Gloria didn't write that one down.

In speaking it aloud, Mack and Gloria could both find where word choice or sentence structure needed tweaking. Practicing with the kids was a way to get a response from fresh ears. Even if they were a quarter the age of most of the actual jury members.

The boys were allowed to play one more race after issuing their opinions on the opening argument. After that, Gloria took Liam home and Mack settled his kids in for the night. He packed up the notes for the case and then took his guitar outside. It was only when he absent-mindedly started strumming a breakup song that he realized Melissa hadn't called to wish the kids goodnight.

He wondered if he should call her. Would that seem like he was checking up on her? Was he? They were divorced, but with the kids, they were still a family, and it was still kind of his responsibility to make sure Ava and Dev's mom was okay. If he'd thought of this when the kids were getting ready for bed, he wouldn't be in this conundrum. Now it was too late to have one of them call her. He'd send a text. Just an update on the kids.

He set aside the guitar and took out his phone: *Both reported school was 'good.' Dev had Liam over tonight while Gloria and I worked on the case.*

He sent it and went back to playing his guitar. An hour and a half later, her response came in: *Good good. Sorry I couldn't call tonight. Out with Martin.*

That explained it. Still, she couldn't have taken a break to call?

PART II

The Trial

Chapter 13

No matter how long he prepared for a case, months or years, Mack always had that same tension race through him on the first day of a new trial. Ava had chosen his dark gray suit and his blue diamond tie when he'd asked her opinion the night before. Blue was always a solid choice. It made people believe you were trustworthy, according to those who bought into the color theory stuff, which Antonia did. Antonia also read him his horoscope that morning before they went to the courthouse. Mack didn't put stock in that sort of thing, but it didn't hurt to have the confidence boost of her positive words.

He had been here yesterday, of course, for the jury selection, but it still felt different when he walked in. The wood rails and floor seemed shinier.

At the courthouse café, he met with the class representatives who would be taking the stand that day. He did final prep with them over coffee so every detail would be fresh as they took their turns before the jury and judge. A couple hours later, they all entered the courtroom and took their seats, awaiting the entrance of the jury and Judge Keats. Mack noted the entire team of lawyers taking up the Polson Reed table. There were four lawyers, and five paralegals seated behind them. Mack had Gloria and Antonia. The visuals were intimidating, but that was part of their game.

It wasn't long before the jury and judge entered. Formal beginnings out of the way, Mack was invited to launch into his opening statement.

"Ladies and gentlemen, Polson Reed Trucking has made repeated, unequivocal statements in the course of this case, and in the end, it's all going to come down to math. These truck drivers are paid through an Activity-Based Compensation scheme. Months ago, when this all began, I asked one of Polson Reed's employees—one they put forth as knowledgeable about their pay calculation methods—what the route pay was for. He told us it was for the work the drivers did before and after their shifts, which according to him, accounted for about an hour and a half of work.

This was from Ed Schmidt. He wasn't the only one to say this either. You'll hear the same from their operations manager and another driver manager. The route pay is thirty dollars for one and a half hours of work done before and after shifts.

"I'm going to show you evidence from the defendants' own lawyers that they've been telling the judge one thing and they're going to tell you something different during this trial. Just before we came to trial, Polson Reed designated three people to speak for the company. They're going to tell you that route pay was not just for the pre- and post-shift work, but that it was also meant to compensate for rest breaks required by law to be provided to the drivers. You smart folks are going to see that the math just doesn't work out.

"When we first asked how the route pay was calculated, everyone pointed us to Ed Schmidt. They said, 'Ask him, he knows.'" Mack spread his arms. "Mr. Schmidt stated very clearly that they observed the drivers and did a survey. The results showed it took around forty-five minutes to complete pre-shift work and another forty-five minutes to complete post-shift work. Mr. Schmidt told us the pay for those tasks was calculated at twenty dollars per hour. An hour and a half times twenty dollars an hour...I don't need to tell you that makes thirty dollars. That's the entire value of the route pay. There's no money left to cover rest breaks."

Mack shook his head. "These three people they've brought in to testify in this trial are going to say the route pay covers pre-shift work, post-shift work, and rest breaks. That's a big load for thirty dollars, and they have no documentation to back it up. I've been through their handbook and their collective bargaining agreement, which, by the way, is one hefty read. Took me almost a week to get through it." He caught a small smile from the accountant. "I've been through all of that material, and so has my associate. Not once is route pay mentioned. There is nothing about payment for rest breaks. Hundreds of thousands of records and no route pay for rest breaks.

"Ladies and gentlemen, this is wage theft." Mack punctuated the statement by driving his pointer finger into his other palm. "Polson Reed isn't stealing from their drivers in one fell swoop. It's more subtle. This multimillion-dollar company is stealing wages from their drivers in ten-, twenty-, and thirty-minute increments every single day, every single shift." He met the passive eyes of the jury. "Maybe that doesn't seem like a lot when you hear it like that, but this is happening with every single driver, and it goes back years. We can only reach back eight years to reclaim what's been taken from these men and women, but it is their money.

"These are hard workers. They're not here to win the lottery or fund retirement for the rest of their lives. They are here to ask to be paid for the work they've already done. They're here to reclaim what's owed to them. It hardly seems fair that they have to go through all this trouble to do it. They're relying on you to see to it that the law is upheld, and their wages are returned to them."

Mack closed by meeting the eyes of each juror and then resumed his seat. After speeches like that, he always had an urge to let out a huge sigh, but that would be a mistake. Now that they were in this courtroom, with their audience of six jurors, there was no taking the game face off. Mack waited until Aaron Norris had the juror's attention before taking a sip from his water glass—the only way to come down off the adrenaline.

Aaron's opening statements were going as expected. He stated how well the drivers were paid. "Some make over eighty thousand dollars a year, and they have a lot of downtime waiting for trucks to be unloaded. They spend that time on their phones, or chatting with other drivers, clowning around. They have nothing to do for a fair amount of each shift. On top of that, these drivers do not record their time properly."

Mack had expected this accusation as it had come up during depositions. He didn't turn his head to scan the drivers seated behind him, but he knew a few of them would be balling their hands into fists. They had gone over this, and Mack would have his chance to show that the managers were the ones insisting on fudging the numbers on the logs.

Norris moved toward his conclusion and then he made a motion that started Mack's heart racing.

"As the videotapes of the depositions mischaracterize the testimony of witnesses who will testify in person, the deposition testimonies are not relevant."

Without those tapes, their side could make any claims they wanted about how the route pay was calculated. Without those tapes, Ed Schmidt could change his calculation claims. Without those tapes, Mack's opening statement could be perceived as lies or misinterpretation of the facts as presented by Polson Reed's esteemed employees.

Mack balled his hand into a fist to keep himself from raking it through his hair. He schooled his face and watched as Aaron Norris presented his motion to exclude all Poyfair Law's evidence.

Judge Keats listened patiently, but it didn't take him long to dismiss the motion. "Mr. Poyfair gets to cross-examine your clients with any and everything he has. That's the whole point of prosecution. If one of his clients says something contradictory, you get to question that as well."

Mack didn't let the relief show. It had been an absurd shot in the dark from Norris's side, but Mack had seen the briefs from the Humbert Lewis law team. They could spin straw into gold.

Norris accepted the judge's ruling and went back to his table for a moment before calling the first witness. "Rudy Weber."

Rudy was the opposition's Aubrey. He was introduced by his credentials—a recent MIT graduate, and he looked like it. He started spinning numbers and formulas used throughout the United States to calculate wages. Rudy pulled out a report and a chart showing how he calculated the salary of every truck driver, including the rest breaks.

"And then what did you do?" asked Norris.

"I took the average of all the work that was done using a survey and divided it by the number of drivers we had. I came out with a ratio. Using that ratio, I was able to calculate the amount of wages due."

"What did the results tell you?"

"The Polson Reed drivers are being paid properly."

"Thank you," Norris said.

Mack rose to do his cross-examination. "Mr. Weber, you've just outlined what appears to be a pretty thorough compensation plan."

He smiled. "I am pretty smart, and I did go to MIT."

"I heard," Mack said. "These formulas you have are pretty important?"

"Yes," he said.

"They comprise the compensation scheme used by Polson Reed?"

"Yes."

"Do you use these same formulas to calculate wages across any state?"

"Similar ones, but each state has its own wage laws, so the formulas change a little."

"And you just keep all these formulas in your head? They're not written down anywhere?"

"No. They're all kept in my mind." The kid smiled again and jutted his chin forward.

Mack smiled back. "How many drivers did you enter into the formula for California?"

The kid looked unsure. "I don't know that off the top of my head."

"How much time in your complicated formula did you assign for pre-shift work?"

He frowned. "What do you mean?"

"How long did it take the driver to complete pre-shift work?"

"I'm not really sure. We talked to a driver."

"No one ever asked that driver what the job duties were for pre-shift?"

The kid scratched his head. "I assume getting ready for work."

Mack nodded. "Right. I got ready for work too. I put on a suit. What do the drivers have to do?"

"I guess put on clothes too?"

Mack smiled. "Yes, but what activities do they need to do? Do they check the safety of the truck? Fill out forms? Do you know how long it takes to fill out the forms? This stuff would have been important to your complicated calculations. Did you do any of those?"

There was a pause. "No."

"So where did you get the number you needed for that part of the formula? Where did you get the one-point-five?" Mack pointed to it on the report Rudy had provided.

"I got that estimate from the company, from someone who works with the drivers."

"And who was that?"

"Ed Schmidt."

"Thank you, Rudy. No further questions."

Chapter 14

The defense called Kayleen Lucas next, from Polson Reed's HR department. After swearing in, she let out a hacking smoker's cough. Mack swore he could see phlegm hit the floor in front of the witness stand. Norris stepped forward, right into the spittle.

"Ms. Lucas, what is your position with Polson Reed?"

"I'm the director of HR, human resources," she rasped. She cleared her throat into her fist.

"Are you involved with payroll?"

She raised a single, over-plucked eyebrow. "That's basically all I do. We're not a touchy-feely company where HR conducts therapy sessions for their employees."

"Right," said Norris. "Can you tell us about the drivers' pay? What do they get paid for?"

"To drive," she said. "Though they also end up with a lot of downtime, it seems. I swear sometimes we pay them just to goof off."

"How do you mean?"

"I've seen a lot of those drivers shooting the breeze at a drop-off, chatting with the store owners. Some of them have no work ethic whatsoever and their work histories show it."

"Can you give an example?"

Ms. Lucas started attacking various class representatives, claiming they were often late or unnecessarily slow on deliveries.

"I see," said Norris. "So they are paid for all this wasted time?"

"They aren't the most honest bunch, you know. I'm sure they fudge their logs enough."

After the depositions, Mack and Gloria had been prepared for these character attacks and weren't at all fazed by it.

"Can you tell us what is factored into the drivers' pay? What elements determine how much they get paid?"

"Oh, sure," she said. Her shoulders straightened. It was obvious to Mack that she felt more prepared for this. "The miles they drive are a large component. In addition, there's the route pay."

"What does the route pay account for?"

"The route pay accounts for pre-shift and post-shift work, as well as the paid rest breaks required by the state of California."

Mack shared a side glance with Gloria. She just barely flicked her eyebrows up for a second.

"Their pre-shift and post-shift work along with the rest breaks are factored into the route pay?" Norris parroted.

"That's correct."

"And that is accounted for in Mr. Weber's calculations?"

"Of course. I provided him with some of the information he needed for his formulas."

The rest of Norris's questioning pursued this same information, repeating the supposed fact that the route pay covered rest breaks in addition to the pre-shift and post-shift work. Mack was completely unconcerned. They had Ed's deposition, which would contradict this with his insistence that the hours were calculated for pre-shift and post-shift work. When Norris was done, Mack stepped forward to whittle away at Ms. Lucas's insistence.

"Ms. Lucas, you said you're the director of human resources?"

"Yes," she confirmed.

"Can you give us a brief explanation of what that role means?" Mack asked.

She scratched one of her hands, probably jonesing for a cigarette based on the cough and her yellowed nails. "I'm in charge the entire human resources," she said.

"Human resources, that would be every human at the company, correct?"

"Yes. Every human."

"And you're in charge of the compensation that is paid?"

She glanced at Norris and then said, "Well, there's more that goes into it than that. We have benefits and such that also contribute to compensation plans."

"Right," Mack said, redirecting her before she could take the questioning off course. "But part of your job is communicating these compensation plans to employees, correct?"

"Yes."

"You said the route pay was very simple. That it pays for the pre-shift work, the post-shift work, and the rest breaks. But this isn't written down anywhere, is it?"

Her lips pressed together for a second. "No, I guess not."

"If that is the case, how do you know this is true?"

"Corporate factored in the rest breaks."

"But if there's no documentation, how were the drivers informed that the route pay was for rest breaks?"

Her scratching hand stopped, and her eyes shifted around for a few seconds. After a silence long enough to show she had no response, Mack said, "No further questions."

Norris came up for the rebuttal and asked, "You are part of the onboarding process for new employees, correct?"

"They meet with me, yes."

"Do you discuss compensation at those meetings?"

"Of course."

"And the route pay would be discussed as part of that conversation?"

"Yes. It is a part of the drivers' compensation so it would come up."

"And the items that the route pay covers would be addressed?"

"Yes," said Ms. Lucas.

"So it is possible that you have verbally communicated to all the drivers employed by Polson Reed that their route pay accounts for rest breaks, as well as the pre- and post-shift work?"

"Yes."

"Thank you, Ms. Lucas," said Norris. Kayleen Lucas was excused from the witness stand.

Norris called Duane Frederick forward, an older Teamster. In the course of his questioning by the defense, it was clear that Norris was still trying to suggest the rest breaks were preempted, but this time under the Labor Management Relations Act. Mack was ready to push back and refocus on the point that separate payment was required by the state of California and Polson Reed had no record of rest breaks being paid separately.

"Mr. Frederick," Mack began, "are you familiar with Polson Reed's payment methods in this particular case?"

"Yes."

"Were you present during the contract negotiations where route pay was discussed?"

"Yes."

Mack led him through setting the scene a little, making sure that Ed Schmidt's name came out as also being present at the negotiations.

Mack presented a statement from Ed Schmidt. "Here you can see a declaration by Mr. Schmidt that in those negotiations of the route pay, it was agreed by the union and Polson Reed that drivers spent approximately an hour and a half on pre-shift and post-shift work and that thirty dollars per day was fair compensation for that time. Do you remember that agreement?"

"I don't. It was a long time ago, however."

"I see. What is your understanding of the purpose of the route pay? What is it meant to compensate for?" Mack asked.

"The pre-shift and post-shift work you mentioned. I don't remember how much time or the amount, but I do remember that we agreed on route pay for the extra time for each shift."

"Was there any statement regarding the route pay being separate compensation for rest breaks?"

"No, there wasn't."

"At these negotiations, anything officially discussed and agreed upon would be reduced to writing, would it not?"

"Yes."

"If a major item was agreed upon, would there be any reason it would not go in writing?" Mack asked.

"No, that's the whole point. We're there negotiating the CBA. If the agreement isn't written up at the end, then what was the point of it all?" Frederick said.

"Where in the CBA does it say that route pay is for rest breaks?"

After a weighty pause, Mr. Frederick said, "It doesn't."

Mack kept his face neutral. "To your knowledge, was there ever separate compensation paid to the drivers in this case for rest breaks?"

"Nothing separate from the activity-based compensation."

"Thank you, Mr. Frederick."

Norris was on his feet for the redirect before Mack even sat down. "Mr. Frederick, is there any physical record of what was discussed at these negotiations?"

"There's the CBA, the collective bargaining agreement."

"The CBA is the final outcome of the negotiations, correct?" Norris asked.

"Yes."

"It isn't a record of all the things discussed in detail at the meeting?"

"No."

"Is there any record of that sort?" Norris pressed.

"Some of us take notes," Frederick said.

"Do you have any of those notes?"

"It's possible I have some stored away somewhere."

"Have you recently looked for those notes?"

"No."

"But you specifically recall having the route pay discussion eleven years ago? Or do you simply think you probably discussed it?"

"We discussed it. I don't necessarily recall all the specific conversations or what was said, but we absolutely talked about the route pay."

"Since you don't have notes and you don't recall all of the specifics of the conversation, isn't it possible that there was talk of the rest periods within the conversation about route pay?"

Frederick scratched his head, either thinking through the question or trying to draw up a more precise memory of the negotiations. "It is possible."

"How many meetings would you have had to arrive at the CBA?"

"I suppose around six or seven. It's always several, never less than five," said Frederick.

"Was Ed Schmidt present for all of those meetings?"

"I couldn't say for certain."

"How long does it take to do pre-shift work?" Norris asked.

"We originally determined it was supposed to be an hour for pre-shift and then fifteen minutes for the post."

"What about the other fifteen minutes?" Norris asked.

Mack felt something sink inside him.

"There was no other fifteen minutes. It was an hour and fifteen total."

"Did you negotiate for an hour and a half for route pay activities?" Norris asked, his body opening toward the jury.

"I don't remember an hour and a half being—"

"You saw the declaration Mr. Poyfair showed where Ed Schmidt referenced that amount of time."

"Yes."

"That's what you and the others discussed at the negotiations, isn't it?"

"No. We discussed an hour and fifteen."

"Mr. Schmidt said the route pay covered an hour and a half of time per shift, calculated at a rate of twenty dollars per hour. You say that the pre-shift and post-shift time was calculated at an hour and fifteen, so that's an extra fifteen minutes of pay per shift." Norris clasped his hands behind his back. "As you said, it's possible that a discussion of rest break pay fell under the conversation regarding route pay. Does it seem reasonable to you that this fifteen-minute discrepancy between your recollection and Mr. Schmidt's deposition covers the rest breaks?"

Frederick pondered for a moment, looking up at the courthouse ceiling a great distance away. "It does seem possible," he said at last.

"Thank you, Mr. Frederick."

Judge Keats dismissed Duane Frederick and Norris called his final witness for the day: Lucy Vandercamp, VP of Compensation Benefits for the sister corporation to Polson Reed. Even though Kayleen Lucas had worn a similar pantsuit, the difference between the two women was distinct. Lucy Vandercamp carried herself with certain expectations. She was obviously corporate and accustomed to the luxuries that came with higher pay. Her pantsuit looked professionally pressed whereas Ms. Lucas's had held some creases from recent purchase. Lucy Vandercamp's hair was straight and shiny while Kayleen Lucas's had been slightly frizzy waves.

"Ms. Vandercamp, how does your position relate to the operations at Polson Reed?" Norris asked.

"We provide guidance on compensation and benefits for all the companies in our organization."

Norris went on to establish her background—including a legal education and her impressive work history—to validate her expertise. Then he got to the same message he'd been hammering at from the start of the day: "Ms. Vandercamp, as vice president of compensation, you must have a strong comprehension of all that goes into the compensation packages for the various employees of Polson Reed. Do you agree with that?"

"I would say that's true, yes."

"Can you tell us what the route pay section of the Polson Reed drivers' paychecks accounts for?"

"The route pay, as I understand it, compensates drivers for pre-shift activities, post-shift activities, and rest breaks."

Mack took note and met eyes with Gloria for a moment. Sometimes semantics mattered more than people thought.

"Thank you, Ms. Vandercamp," said Norris.

Mack opened his cross-examination by targeting her last remark. "I was listening very carefully and you said, 'as I understand it.' Now, how did you come to this understanding of what route pay entails? Was there documentation that indicated route pay is separate compensation for the rest breaks?"

"The information concerning rest breaks is included in the wage progression PowerPoint presentation we provided."

"The PowerPoint presentation told you that route pay covers rest breaks for the drivers?"

"It says we pay for rest breaks for our warehouse employees," Ms. Vandercamp stated.

Mack noticed her careful phrasing, but he had to point it out to the jury. He knew that PowerPoint presentation backward and forward, as he knew all their onboarding materials. It would show what she was saying, but it would also show that it didn't account for the drivers.

"Let's pull up that PowerPoint deck. Plaintiffs' Exhibit Number Five." The presentation appeared on the screen provided by the court. "Is this the PowerPoint presentation you're talking about?"

"Yes," she confirmed.

"Can you show us where it says that route pay is separate compensation for rest breaks?"

"It says rest breaks are separate compensation on slide twenty-one."

Obligingly, Mack had the slides advanced. "This is slide twenty-one, correct?"

"Yes."

"Where does it say that route pay is separate compensation for rest breaks?"

Ms. Vandercamp sighed at him. He knew that she had never claimed it said a word about route pay, but it was important to point this out.

"It doesn't say 'route pay,'" she said. "I said that it indicates paid rest breaks for warehouse employees."

"This is solely for warehouse workers. It's not for truck drivers, is it?" Mack asked.

"That's exactly what I said." Ms. Vandercamp pressed her lips into a line.

"So where did you come to your understanding that route pay is separate compensation for rest breaks for drivers?" Mack asked again. "Did anyone ever *tell* you that route pay was separate compensation for rest breaks?"

"No one has said that to me."

"Did Ed Schmidt ever say that?"

"No, not to me. He and I have scarcely ever spoken."

"What about Duane Frederick? Has he ever said that route pay compensates drivers for their rest breaks?"

"Not to me, no."

Mack displayed the transcripts of Ed Schmidt's deposition. "Here is what general manager Ed Schmidt said regarding route pay: 'Polson Reed and the union agreed that route pay compensates drivers for pre-shift and post-shift activities. It was agreed that drivers spend an average of one and a half hours on those activities combined. Route pay at the rate of thirty dollars per day was agreed to be a fair and accurate amount to compensate drivers for the pre-shift and post-shift work.' Do you see these words?"

"Yes."

"Do you agree that is the policy of Polson Reed Trucking?"

"I can't speak to that."

"Do the words 'rest break' appear in that statement?"

"I don't know if he mentioned it elsewhere in his statement, but in that section, no, those words are not present."

Mack presented another document. "In this statement by a Polson Reed attorney, they say that under the activity-based compensation system, otherwise known as ABC, drivers are paid for three components—miles, pallets, and stops. Do you agree with this?"

"I can't say for certain what the three components are."

"Polson Reed never said these three components covered pre-shift and post-shift work. Have they ever stated that?"

"I don't know what Polson Reed Trucking has stated regarding the components of the ABC system."

"In fact, they specifically negotiated route pay as a separate, fourth component of the ABC pay to cover the pre- and post-shift work. Are you aware of that?"

"I have not seen the collective bargaining agreement that established route pay."

"But you're aware that there is a fourth component to the route pay?"

"I do not have a working definition of route pay."

"You don't have a definition of route pay?"

"That's what I just said."

"Then why did you claim it covered the pre-shift, post-shift, and rest breaks?"

"That's my understanding of it."

"You weren't part of the negotiations concerning the CBA, correct?"

"No."

"And so you weren't part of the negotiations for route pay, correct?"

"I was not."

"And you didn't have a conversation with anyone to come to that understanding of it, correct?"

"I have not had a conversation about route pay."

"You have not produced a single document that says route pay is separate compensation for rest breaks, right?"

"None that referenced route pay specifically, no."

"The testimony I have shown you from Ed Schmidt and the Polson Reed attorney shows that they both said the route pay was for pre-shift and post-shift work only, right?"

"It reads that way," Ms. Vandercamp hedged.

"One final thing, this is a compensation plan for drivers." Mack produced the exhibit. "It references a mileage rate, correct?"

"I see a mileage rate here," she concurred.

"And a stop rate?"

"Yes."

"And a route pay description is there?"

"Yes."

With satisfaction, Mack noted a tightening along her jawline. "It mentions pre- and post-shift, but no rest breaks, right?"

"The words 'rest break' do not appear on this document."

"Do you know why none of the documents we've looked at say that route pay is separate compensation for rest breaks?"

"No, I do not."

"Last question. Do you know how the drivers in this case are paid for their rest breaks?"

"I do not know what appears on their paychecks."

Mack nodded once. "No further questions."

*

Mack managed to make it out of court in time to watch the end of Dev's first basketball practice. The coach was apparently one of the parents and seemed a little overwhelmed at coaching twenty ten-year-olds. In fact, Mack wasn't convinced that the poor father knew much about basketball at all, other than the basics of scoring and the most obvious penalties.

He didn't seem to know how to set up a play at all. The kids were rampaging from one end of the gym to the other with the basketball and with no clear directions. It looked more like a game of keep-away than basketball practice.

Having played a bit in high school, Mack was quite familiar with the sport and had even taken a leading role on his college intramural team. When the coach blew his whistle precisely at four-thirty, Dev came over to Mack with less energy than Mack had expected.

"What's up, bud?" Mack asked when Dev didn't greet him.

"Nothin'," said Dev. "Let's go."

Minutes later, they were in the car on the way to Melissa's, and Dev was still silent.

"What's going on, Dev?" Mack asked. "Is basketball not as much fun as you thought it would be?"

"I don't know." Dev shrugged and kicked his backpack, which sat on the floor in front of him. "It doesn't feel like I'm playing a game. It just feels like I'm running." He made a face at Mack.

"Yeah? It did seem like maybe your coach wasn't too sure of himself."

"Coach Ingram is just Bo's dad. He never even played basketball," Dev said.

That had been obvious to Mack. "Oh yeah? How come he's the coach then?"

"I guess no one else wanted to." Mack could feel Dev's side-eye. "You played basketball when you were in school, right?"

"Yeah, I did."

"I think you should be our coach," Dev said. "We're gonna get killed if we play against teams with real coaches."

"I don't want to take Coach Ingram's job away from him," Mack said.

Dev's eyes brightened and he wiggled in the passenger seat. "It's not his job. He builds houses or something. He said someone else would be coaching us next week."

"Maybe they will be a better coach," Mack said.

"No. It's gonna be Brady's dad."

Mack blinked. "Are they just cycling through the parents?"

Dev nodded.

"I wasn't asked."

"Mom said you were busy with a case."

Mack frowned. "You're never going to learn the game if you always have a different coach and none of them ever teach you any strategy."

"You could teach us strategy," Dev said.

Mack twisted his hands around the steering wheel a little. "You know," he said, "I think I'll call the school and see if they want a more permanent basketball coach for the fourth-grade team."

Dev grinned and pumped his fist in the air. "Yeah!"

That was enough of a win for the day that Mack didn't need to dwell on the progress of the trial. He chuckled as the thought occurred to him that Jack would be happy to hear he was branching out.

Chapter 15

oday was Mack's turn to control the narrative. Although yesterday had gone rather well, he still felt the trial nerves. It didn't help that when he had combed his hair that morning, a veritable shower of hairs fell onto the counter. Their first witness would be Amanda Bronson, the seventeen-year driver who had been fired during the course of the lawsuit. Gloria had prepped Amanda for this. Amanda had one of the longest employment records with Polson Reed out of all the drivers, and she was an extremely composed person. Mack was anticipating her being one of the strongest voices for the drivers.

After she was sworn in, Mack began. "Mrs. Bronson, how long did you work for Polson Reed?"

"It was about seventeen years."

"Have you always been a driver while you worked there?"

"Yes." She smiled warmly, like the mother she was.

"Can you briefly describe how you were paid?"

"Sure thing. There's route pay, piece count, and by stops and miles. That's all we're paid."

"You mentioned route pay. What's your understanding of what that includes?"

"It pays us for the paperwork and stuff we need to do before our trips and after them. The time it takes for that."

"How did you arrive at that understanding?"

"Ed Schmidt said it at one of our driver meetings."

"Do remember when that was?"

She shook her head. "Can't say for sure."

Mack knew that answer was coming, like all the answers he was getting, but still he asked the questions. "Do you remember what Ed Schmidt told you about route pay at that meeting?"

"He just said that route pay would be for our paperwork time, the work we do pre-trip and post-trip."

"Thank you, Mrs. Bronson."

Aaron Norris allowed his associate, Cassidy Perkins to do the cross this time. She stood and strode forward, square heels clonking on the floor with authority.

"Mrs. Bronson, has anyone at Polson Reed ever told you route pay did *not* compensate you for your rest breaks?"

"Nobody every explained anything to us regarding rest breaks. I was only told that route pay would be for pre-shift, post-shift, and paperwork. That's all."

"Did you ever ask Mr. Schmidt whether route pay covered your rest breaks as well?"

"No."

"So you don't know whether or not rest breaks were included in your route pay?"

"I was told it was only for pre- and post-shift paperwork."

"Nobody said that it did *not* include rest breaks?"

"We were never told that we were supposed to get paid separately for rest breaks."

"But you understood that meal and rest breaks were your right as an employee, correct?"

"Not until recently, actually."

Perkins stumbled a moment. "You heard the testimony of Ms. Lucas, correct?"

Amanda nodded. "I did."

"She stated that she verbally informed drivers that route pay was for rest breaks. You heard that?"

"I heard it."

"So during your onboarding as a driver for Polson Reed, she informed you that route pay included payment for your rest breaks. Isn't that right?"

"Kayleen Lucas didn't even start working for Polson Reed until nine years after I did. She couldn't have told me."

Perkins's mouth went flat and the corners of her eyes pinched. "No further questions."

Driver after driver was brought forward and testified to the same facts: There was no separate pay for rest breaks, and route pay was only ever claimed to cover pre-shift and post-shift work.

Finally, it was time to call up Ed Schmidt. Mack had found it a little difficult getting the man to court. The defense claimed to not know where he was for a time, and he had pretended to be on vacation. Mack had been forced to hire someone to track down Schmidt and serve him with the subpoena. He was here now, thank goodness. It was time to catch Schmidt in his own tangled web of words.

Mack ran through the introductory bits, letting Schmidt tell the court about his experience with Polson Reed and the drivers. Then he started in on Schmidt's deposition and declaration, which had been submitted to the court already.

"You stated that Polson Reed and the union agreed upon route pay that would compensate drivers for their pre- and post-shift work. Do you recall saying that?" Mack asked.

"Yes."

"You were present at those negotiations, correct?"

"Yes."

"In your declaration, you wrote that the negotiations of the route pay led to an agreement that one and a half hours were spent on pre- and post-shift work for the drivers. Is that right?"

"Yes."

"Is that a true statement? That one and a half hours account for pre- and post-shift work?"

"Yes."

"You also stated that thirty dollars was calculated for the route pay based on a twenty-dollar-per-hour base rate and the hour and a half time estimation. Is that right?"

"Yes."

"That thirty dollars was meant as compensation for the one and a half hours of pre- and post-shift work, correct?"

Ed Schmidt's irritation at this repetition was plain in his snappish, "Yes."

"In your declaration, you listed the activities included in pre-shift and post-shift work." Mack directed him to the appropriate paragraph of his declaration. "For example, here you list a pre-trip meeting, truck and trailer inspection, load verification and inspection, and route paperwork. Are those the activities for pre-shift work?"

"Yes, as an example."

"And for post-shift, you mentioned parking, post-trip inspection, paperwork, cleaning the trucks, and registering any problems with the truck. Is that accurate?"

"Again, as an example, yes."

"And route pay covers all these activities? And nothing else?"

"Those are things they have to do for every shift, but there can sometimes be more items, if there are problems with the truck or the load."

"Is there any way that the post-trip tasks could be done competently in fifteen minutes?"

"Fifteen minutes?"

"Based on your experience as a manager supervising dozens to hundreds of drivers, could the post-shift tasks be completed in fifteen minutes?"

"Why are you asking about fifteen minutes? What does that have to do with anything?"

"I asked you a question."

"Fine. No. They couldn't do all that in fifteen minutes. Not properly."

A pleasant chord of music slipped through Mack's mind. Ed Schmidt would nail this case to the wall for him. "How long would you say it would take?"

"Thirty to forty-five minutes."

"That's why you negotiated for an hour and a half, correct?"

"Yes."

"Route pay did not include separate compensation for rest breaks, isn't that right?"

"Route pay covered all the activities mentioned in paragraph six of my declaration."

"And rest breaks are not mentioned in that paragraph?"

"Route pay was part of the hour and a half to pay for pre- and post-shift work."

Judge Keats interrupted. "You must answer yes or no to that question please."

Through gritted teeth, Schmidt said, "No."

"Thank you," said Mack. "Route pay was for nothing other than the pre- and post-shift tasks, correct?"

"It was for the hour and a half of activity before and after shifts," said Schmidt.

Mack pressed the point. "And nothing else?"

"And nothing else," Schmidt affirmed.

"Mr. Schmidt, did you ever talk with Kayleen Lucas about route pay?"

"Yeah."

"What did you say?"

"Just what I told you. What the pay is for."

"Did you ever tell Kayleen Lucas that route pay compensated for rest breaks?"

Schmidt frowned. "I'm not sure I remember that."

"Do you remember telling her that route pay was connected with rest breaks?"

"Route pay includes what I told you before."

"I want to know if you ever had a conversation with Kayleen Lucas about what the route pay entails. Yes or no?"

"I told you yes."

"And did that conversation include a discussion of rest breaks being part of route pay? Yes or no?"

Mack could see a muscle jump in Schmidt's jaw. "No."

"You held a meeting with the drivers to explain route pay, correct?"

"Yes."

"And you told them that route pay was for their pre-shift and post-shift tasks?"

"Yes."

"You didn't mention rest breaks as part of the route pay?"

"I explained that the routing they receive is inclusive of route pay and every component associated with that, and their meals and breaks were in the routing."

Mack's guts twisted. This slippery fish was trying to wiggle back to the narrative of everything being lumped together. He needed to show the jury that this man wasn't here to clarify anything, but rather to back anything and everything the company said, true or not.

"Why would you tell them the meals and breaks were in the routing?"

"It's important that they understand what's in the route packet."

"Mr. Schmidt, you testified that route pay was not separate compensation for rest breaks. Do you recall that?"

"Yes, of course." His blond brows pulled down to create a heavier brow line.

"Why would you tell drivers that route pay includes their rest breaks if that isn't true?" Mack asked.

"Route pay is part of the ABC plan."

"What does that have to do with the rest breaks?" Mack asked. It was infuriating the way Ed Schmidt kept trying to skirt around questions. As crucial as Schmidt's testimony was to Mack's case, trying to extract a straight answer from the man was exhausting.

"Meals and breaks are built into the routes the drivers bid on."

"'Built in' doesn't mean the same thing as separately compensated, does it?" Mack asked.

"It's part of the pay."

"The thirty dollars was meant to pay for an hour and a half of pre-shift and post-shift work, right?" Mack pressed.

"Yes."

"How is there anything left to pay for rest breaks?" There was a long silence. "No further questions at this time," Mack said.

A brief recess was called.

"Good God," Gloria said. "Could that man be any more difficult?"

Mack shrugged. "I think we got our point across despite his attempts at misdirection. If nothing else, he at least seems untrustworthy." Mack checked his phone and remembered his conversation with Dev last night. Mack said, "I need to go call Dev's school. Back in a second."

The call was brief, and the athletic director was thrilled by Mack's offer to volunteer. Mack made it clear that he didn't want to take the position from anyone, but that Dev had mentioned maybe they needed an actual coach.

"I can guarantee the parents will be relieved," the athletic director said. "I think the kids will be too."

"I'm happy to do it. Can I just have you send over the game schedule and the practice times to my email address?"

"Absolutely. We should have that on file," she said. She confirmed the email address with him, and they said good-bye.

As much as Mack felt he should be focusing on building up his fledgling law practice, there had been enough quiet nights alone at home to convince him that he had room for other commitments in his life.

Court reconvened and Norris began his cross-examination, running through several sections of Schmidt's deposition where he said things like, 'Route pay compensates for pre-shift and post-shift and anything in between.'

"What does that mean, 'anything in between,' Mr. Schmidt?" Norris asked.

"The ILD routing."

Norris directed his attention to Defense Exhibit 24. "Is this an example of an industrial logistics design routing manual, or 'ILD' as you just referred to it?" he asked.

"Yes."

"You had one of these at the time of the negotiations regarding route pay?"

"Yes."

"How frequently did you receive these ILD routing manuals?"

"Every time we did a reroute, about once or twice a year."

"To your knowledge, have they always looked like this?"

"Yes."

"Along the top, has it always had the terms 'pre-shift,' 'post-shift,' and 'rest break?'"

"As far as I know, yes."

"No further questions, Your Honor."

Schmidt looked incredibly relaxed now, but his posture changed two seconds later when Mack stood up to conduct his redirect. "You said route pay is part of the activity-based compensation?"

"That's right," said Schmidt.

"And as Mr. Norris pointed out, you indicated it covers pre-shift and post-shift and the activities in between, yes?"

"That's correct."

"Rest breaks, though, are defined by the lack of activity, are they not? Drivers shouldn't be doing any activity during that time, right?"

"No."

"Nothing further, Your Honor."

A single other witness was lined up and his testimony was short. He had also been present at the negotiations. He reported recalling the thirty dollars for route pay and no reference to compensating rest breaks. Norris pressed him into saying that he may have been in the bathroom while that piece came up. Mack didn't find it worth his time to dispute that statement and announced he had nothing more to put before the court. Norris stated the same and the court adjourned for a time, not to return until closing statements.

Chapter 16

Mack ate a light lunch before heading back in to do his closing statement. He had found over the years that lighter meals were a better choice during a trial. If he ate his fill of a burrito or a full plate of downhome cooking, he was bound to feel more lethargic. So, a salmon salad was in order. Gloria was the opposite. She always claimed she needed the strength only red meat could offer to keep her sharp. "It's a good source of iron," she told him, digging into a steak. "Iron is critical for cognitive function, memory, and a good attention span. All important for litigating."

"All that's left is the closing statements."

"So what's the problem if I'm weighed down by food?" she challenged.

He didn't say anything more to that. After working with her for over a decade, Mack knew what this really was. Gloria ate like this when she was nervous or uncertain about the outcome of something. She had turned into a ravenous carnivore for the first two weeks after they had left Myer and O'Toole, snacking on beef jerky and slices of ham through nearly every meeting.

"Let's run over the closing statement real quick," Mack suggested.

After they paid their lunch bill, Mack asked Gloria to check his tie and they headed back to court.

*

"Repeated and undisputed statements have been made over the long course of this case," Mack said. "Our original claim included missing wages for pre-shift and post-shift work, but several managers at Polson Reed declared the route pay was compensation for that time. Based on this, the court entered a summary judgment eliminating that substantial claim.

"In the past year, that was the testimony in this case: The route pay portion of the Polson Reed drivers' paychecks compensates them for one and a half hours of pre-shift and post-shift work. Who said this? First, Ed Schmidt, the general manager. Then, Duane Frederick. You've heard and seen this same testimony from several managers at Polson Reed and from members of the Teamsters Union. While preparing for this trial, Polson Reed's lawyers stated this same information in briefs, in motions, and in declarations. All these people agree that route pay compensates the drivers for one and a half hours of pre-shift and post-shift work. There is no money for rest breaks.

"You were presented with a compensation plan for the Polson Reed drivers and nowhere in that plan does it account for rest breaks. You have heard testimony stating that at the meeting where the route pay was established and discussed, there was no implication or statement that it would account for rest breaks. And how could it? It's been established that they used a twenty dollars per hour rate for one and a half hours of pre-shift and post-shift time to calculate the route pay of thirty dollars per shift. Twenty times one point five equals thirty. There's no money left for rest breaks and there was no intention to pay for rest breaks with route pay or with any other type of separate compensation, as California law requires.

"Rudy Weber, Kayleen Lucas, Lucy Vandercamp are brand new witnesses to this case, called in to say that the route pay also covers rest breaks. When they're asked how they know this, or how the route pay was calculated, none of them can say. When they're asked what part of the route pay accounts for rest breaks, they don't know. They don't know how it was determined that rest breaks were built into the route pay. They don't know how or if the drivers are told about that. They don't know how many rest breaks are supposedly accounted for in the route pay. They don't know."

Mack made eye contact with several of the jurors. "There was evidence that warehouse workers are compensated for their rest breaks, so it is clear that Polson Reed understands what the law requires. However, there is no evidence that they pay their drivers for *their* rest breaks, and the money they claim provides this separate compensation is all used up by the pre-shift and post-shift time. Polson Reed does not provide separate compensation to their drivers for their rest breaks. This is wage theft. It may not seem like much, a ten-minute break, but over eight years and hundreds of drivers, it makes a very big difference to these drivers and their families.

"These drivers have put in a lot of time asking their employer to do better. They are not looking for a windfall, something to retire on. They simply want to be paid for the work they have already done."

Mack announced that he was through, and Judge Keats called Aaron Norris forward for his closing.

Norris buttoned his suit jacket and began. "There is really only one question before the court today: Were the drivers paid for their rest breaks? There seem to be competing understandings as to whether the drivers knew how they were being paid or whether they knew what their different pay components were for.

"The simple truth is, we have asked witnesses to remember events that took place over ten years ago when they were in discussions over their collective bargaining agreement. None of these witnesses had notes, and many were only in *some* of the meetings, not all of them. We have no way of knowing what happened in all those meetings. Additionally, it's a bit too much to expect people to remember what was said during multiple meetings over a decade ago. Of course there is some confusion and some disagreement among the witnesses. There is hardly any reliable evidence as to what was discussed at those meetings.

"There has been testimony that route pay compensates for an hour and a half of time. There has been testimony stating that pre-shift was calculated at an hour and post-shift at fifteen minutes. Simple math tells us that there are fifteen minutes worth of route pay time left to account for rest breaks."

Mack made a note to dispute that during his rebuttal.

"Kayleen Lucas, the head of human resources, testified that route pay is intended to cover rest breaks. She said that it would have been covered in the discussion of the payment plan when new drivers went through orientation. Of course she can't recall specifically communicating that to the plaintiffs in this case. It was years ago, and as already stated, remembering back so many years makes it near impossible to know anything with certainty.

"The CBA doesn't break down what the route pay is for. However, the ILD, which is used to calculate their routes, accounts for rest breaks, as well as pre-shift and post-shift. Given this information, and the way the ILD is factored into the payment scheme, it is clear the route costs take into account rest breaks for the drivers. Mr. Weber showed this in his calculations.

"Furthermore, the law does not prevent an employer from creating a nonproductive-time payment category. Mr. Poyfair repeatedly asked to be shown a document where it stated route pay compensated for rest breaks. We do not have one and we knew that. Again, we are asking witnesses to recall discussions from more than ten years ago."The plaintiffs need to prove that Polson Reed has an unlawful pay scheme, but the evidence we presented in that PowerPoint slide deck shows that rest breaks are separately compensated. The ILD clearly illustrates how the company pays the drivers and how it prices their transportation services.

"Thank you. Nothing further."

Again, the two lawyers exchanged positions so Mack could enter his rebuttal. "Code 226.2 very clearly says the pay must be separate for rest periods and nonproductive time. Everybody has claimed that it's a component of the AB compensation scheme. That's illegal. It's not separate compensation.

"Route pay was established to cover pre-shift and post-shift tasks. This was told to us by Polson Reed's very own lawyer. They negotiated this separate component of the drivers' pay for this purpose. The ILD routing manuals don't define route pay as compensation for rest breaks. Witnesses have stated that. The ILD manuals don't discuss compensation at all. They are for pricing routes.

"Their director of human resources was unable to provide a concrete way in which drivers were informed of this supposed pay. Mr. Norris here wants us to believe that she communicated it to them verbally, but many of these drivers were in place before she began working for Polson Reed, so how could she possibly know if they were informed of the components of route pay.

"Time and again we were told that route pay is for pre-shift and post-shift tasks. There's no documentation, but that was their claim, until this lawsuit shifted to rest breaks. Then suddenly there were claims that route pay also covered those. Who knows what else will get added to the list when they're asked about something else? You can't use a single bucket for everything. There must be independent compensation for rest breaks, or it gets watered down as soon as paperwork takes a little longer to finish that shift.

"Testimony has stated that using fifteen minutes to complete post-shift work cannot lead to competent and reliable outcomes. Ed Schmidt declared that the time accounted for by route pay was calculated based on what drivers needed to competently complete their pre-shift and post-shift work.

"Polson Reed is responsible for accurately tracking and paying their drivers for their time. Instead, they stole wages ten minutes at a time for years. The defense spent a great deal of time gutting our claim on pre-shift and post-shift time by declaring that route pay accounted for that. Once that claim was dismissed, we only had rest breaks left, and now, suddenly, route pay somehow compensates for that as well, and the time estimates are different. Ed Schmidt told you that the pre-shift and post-shift work could not be carved down to an hour and fifteen minutes. If it were, the drivers would be taking their 80,000-pound truck onto the highways without proper inspection and that's a danger to all of us. They just can't do what is required of them in that amount of time, so where are the rest breaks being paid for? They aren't, and these drivers are owed that.

"Nothing further."

Mack took his seat and concealed a sigh of relief. Despite the wait for the verdict ahead of him, it was always good to know when he had done all he could, and it was out of his hands for the time being.

*

That evening, Mack, Antonia, and Gloria took the kids miniature golfing. Taking the kids out together had become something of a tradition for them when a case was in deliberation. When it was cold or rainy, they went bowling, but when the weather was nice, it was always miniature golf. If a trial had left them in a particular state of tension, Gloria often suggested a movie instead of the more physical activities, but Mack always appreciated the movement. Antonia was playful with the children and even coaxed Ava into enjoying herself despite the young tween's initial resistance to the outing. Mack, on the other hand, was fighting off the constant urge to stare into space and run numbers through his head.

This case had been expensive, and it wasn't over yet. Even if the verdict swung their way—which Gloria seemed rather confident in—Poyfair Law would have a long wait for the payday. The verdict would merely establish whose side was deemed in the right. There was still plenty to negotiate in terms of the actual settlement. That's what had Mack on edge. He would wait for the verdict and, assuming it came in the next couple days, Mack would hopefully have something in hand to present to Elena. It was time to ask for a little more money from the bank to keep things flowing. A reminder floated through his head that many independent law firms collapsed under bankruptcy in their first years of operation. Mack went to brush a hand through his hair and paused mid-action, remembering his resolution to break that habit.

Gloria tapped his foot with her putter. "Cheer up. I bet in twenty-four hours, we'll have a winning verdict."

His tight smile betrayed his misgivings.

Gloria glanced at the children striding ahead of them to the next hole. "What is it?" she asked.

"Just…money," he said. "The firm is depending on this case."

"This seems like a moment for Antonia." The optimistic member of their team was trooping ahead with the children, however. Gloria said, "She'd tell you that we've probably already won the case and that the money will be here in plenty of time. She'd also tell you we have other cases lined up."

"That's a decent channeling of her."

"Not so hard. Just go the opposite of what I usually think." She smiled.

"Well that took away the positivity," Mack said.

"Don't worry about it. Worry is for work, and tonight, we're playing. And you're not doing very well." She tapped the scorecard she was holding. "Time to get your head in the game."

Mack focused on Dev who was lining up a shot at a castle. He would need to send it across the drawbridge so as not to lose the ball in the moat.

Dev lined up his feet and twisted his toes into the Astroturf as if he was preparing for a pitch in the batting cages rather than putting a golf ball. Despite his preparations portending a massive swing, Dev gave the ball a firm tap that sent it right over the drawbridge. He'd gotten rather good at mini golf in the last couple years.

While Dev and Liam were focused on the hole, Ava stepped back to Mack. "Is Mom on another date tonight?"

"What?" As far as Mack knew, Melissa hadn't told the kids she was dating.

"Mom, is she on another date tonight?"

"What makes you think she's been going on dates?"

Ava raised an eyebrow at him. "We've had a babysitter practically once a week when we're with her and she always puts on makeup those nights before she leaves. Sometimes Dev's friend Shonda comes over with the babysitter."

"Did she tell you she was going on a date?"

"No. She said it's book club, but Shonda's dad told her he was going on a date. It's weird that he always goes on a date when Mom goes to book club, don't you think?"

Mack made a noncommittal sound. Melissa had said she would tell the kids when it became more than a couple dates, and it certainly seemed like more than a couple dates based on Ava's evidence. Still, it didn't seem like he should be the one to tell the kids, or even confirm Ava's suspicions.

"I also present that the only book I've seen Mom reading in all this time is *The Turner House*, and her bookmark has barely moved."

Melissa had always been the kind of reader who preferred one-sitting reads like articles and short stories, but she would often pick up award-winning novels that she read in a leisurely way over the course of an entire year. Sometimes she wouldn't finish them at all. Mack didn't say anything but stared down into his daughter's eyes. Those Nancy Drew novels were making her terrifyingly observant or possibly snoopy.

"Are you not supposed to tell me because she's supposed to?"

Mack raised one shoulder and one side of his mouth.

"Are you dating anyone?"

This question he could answer. "No."

"Are you going to?"

"Probably, someday. I'll tell you though." He pointed toward the castle. "It's your shot."

She gave him a stare for a little longer and then took up her position at the tee.

*

Melissa called to wish the kids a good night just as they were brushing their teeth. Mack mentioned the conversation with Ava to Melissa after the kids had each spoken to her.

"You probably should tell them," he said.

"I told you I would when it got more serious."

"I'm not saying you need to tell them who you're dating, but telling them you are dating will make things less surprising for them when you decide to introduce someone to them. Pretending you're not dating when Ava very much believes you are will only make her feel like you're lying to her." Mack didn't point out that the lying was a fact, not just a feeling. "We don't want to lose her trust in us."

There was a long silence. "Okay. I'll talk to her about it."

"Tell Dev too."

"Excuse me?"

"You should tell Dev too," Mack insisted. "He's barely a year younger than her and deserves to know what she does."

"I will tell them that I am dating." She sighed. "I appreciate you not telling her anything. At least I won't be the bad guy for lying and you the good guy for revealing the truth."

"Of course. We might not be married anymore, but we still need to be on the same team."

*

The next day news of a verdict came through and they all gathered in court again. Many of the drivers were present, and the entire panel of Polson Reed's lawyers were gathered at their table. The jury entered and then Judge Keats. Mack pressed flat palms into his thighs as they all stood and then sat for the reading of the verdict.

Judge Keats read, "The jury foreperson will now read the verdict."

The accountant stood and said, "We have come to the decision that the drivers for Polson Reed are entitled to wages for rest breaks. The route pay does not compensate for the rest breaks, as was claimed after it was established that route pay compensated for pre-shift and post-shift work."

"Very well," said Judge Keats. "This is a violation under PAGA and a violation of the unfair competition law, per the plaintiff's claims. As such, the drivers are entitled to wages and penalties, and Mr. Poyfair is entitled to his fees."

A brief celebration erupted among the plaintiffs and then Judge Keats banged his gavel. "Is there anything further for either side?"

Mack felt a weight fly off his chest. "I just want to thank the court for its time, Your Honor," he said. Judge Keats spared him a nod. The defense's side of the room had Norris speaking hurriedly to several people behind him and the other lawyers gathered there. Nothing was presented to the judge and so court was adjourned. Poyfair Law and their clients hastened out of the courtroom.

Chapter 17

Questions came at Mack from the drivers, regarding when and how much would be paid. He reminded them that while it may seem like winning the case should be the end of it, it was only the mid-point. Despite only twelve drivers being present at the verdict reading, there were over a hundred inquiries from the other drivers who had not opted out of the proceedings. They had heard from those present that Polson Reed had lost. These calls were not unexpected and would pour in over the next week. Having done class-action suits before, he knew this was often the case when the suit was very connected with other members of the class.

The call Mack had not been expecting was from Aaron Norris.

"You did a great job there, Mack. It seems Poyfair Law is really going to take off."

In his mind's eye Mack saw the line of credit balance. "Thanks. It was a big win for us."

"There's some road ahead yet, you know," said Norris.

So this was Norris's game. He was calling to remind Mack that the war wasn't over. Considering the meeting he had scheduled with Elena early next week, he was acutely aware the money wasn't in his pocket yet, and that the amount of money there would be was yet to be determined.

"Don't worry. I'm aware of the road ahead. Well prepared for it, in fact. We've got the road snacks and the map," Mack said.

Norris chuckled. "Well, all right then. I'll be seeing what I can do to throw you all off course. But seriously, excellent work in the trial. It was great to see you in court again."

"I appreciate that. You didn't do half-bad yourself." *Just bad enough,* Mack thought.

They ended the call shortly after, and Mack began assembling the documentation regarding the verdict for his meeting with Elena. With the judge's statement, Mack was hoping Elena would see fit to extend his line of credit just a little further, to pay the rent and the employees for a little longer. Elena herself had called to schedule the meeting, the day after the verdict. As Mack had presented the case to her for the initial line of credit request, he figured she must have been keeping an eye on it somehow and was now wanting to get a lead on when the payment for the line of credit would be coming. She had proposed a lunch meeting, and that lack of formality was a relief to him.

When they met the following Monday, there was a lot of friendly chatting before they got down to business, and Mack made sure to take the lead in that direction.

"Did you hear that we just won the Polson Reed Trucking case?" he began.

"I did, actually."

"I've got the ruling here. You may want to look at that when you have some time." Mack handed her the papers he'd brought along.

"That's great. So your firm is in great shape, huh?" she said. Her close observation even as she sipped from her water glass was enough to tell Mack she was trying to suss out when payment would be rolling in.

"It will be soon enough, but there's a bit of a timeline for getting paid. We're looking at a couple more months pushing toward the actual finish line of the payout." Mack briefly broke down the process.

"The situation is, I'd like to extend my line of credit to a million. We've won the case, so the money is coming, but there's some legwork that needs to go into the final payday. You know what I'm saying? We need more operating money to get to that finish line, in order to get to the money."

Elena nudged a piece of fish across her plate. "I understand what you're saying. Is there any chance the awarded amount will be insufficient?"

"I can keep you fully apprised, and if you read that ruling"—Mack gestured to the papers next to her plate—"you'll see that Judge Keats said Poyfair Law is entitled to payment of all fees. In addition, there's a couple other cases heading into the final phases at this time. I've got a Supreme Court case I'm a part of that's heading into oral arguments. It's a large pharmaceutical case. There are several different lawyers in on it, but the payout on that has very real potential."

Elena set down her fork and skimmed the ruling. "The Supreme Court?"

"Yes," Mack confirmed. He realized he hadn't taken a bite of food in a while and cut a piece of chicken to not appear too invested in her response to his request.

She nodded. "Okay. I think we can do this, since you have already won the case and will be receiving some payment for that. I'll extend your line of credit."

"Thank you, Elena." Mack's optimism bloomed on his face for the remainder of the meal. The extension would see them through, and the payout from Polson Reed, Mack was confident, would be enough to pay off his line of credit and take a tidy chunk to the bank for Poyfair Law's coffers.

*

His last night with the kids that week, Mack took his kids to Jack's home where the other former band members were gathered. Janna brought her daughter, and Frank's three kids were also there with his wife Julia. Jack had the designated rehearsal space for Porsche with a sound-proofed room in his townhome. The adults had brought their instruments. After their night out some months ago, Janna had taken it upon herself to arrange this get-together where they would see if they could all still hang together on a song.

While they were still prepping their instruments, Jack made another appeal. "We still need a strong lead guitar to fill in for some upcoming gigs. She's going to take some time off after the baby is born and we're booked for five weddings and a few bar mitzvahs."

"You really need to start looking elsewhere. You'll see after we play a little. I'm not where I need to be for a performance."

"A little practice will take care of that. Besides, you won your trucking case."

Mack felt his confidence swell a little with that mention. Poyfair Law was on its way now, with a solid victory and a case headed to the Supreme Court.

"Why don't you check back with me after the pharma case I have at the Supreme Court. We're doing arguments next week."

"Supreme Court, huh? Lah-di-dah. You're in the big time now, huh?" Jack nudged him.

Mack grinned.

Some of the kids were settled in front Jack's bachelor big-screen TV with a movie, Dev among them. Ava had parked herself in a corner of the rehearsal room with a book, but when they started playing, she placed her bookmark and listened as though the concert was for her alone. Eventually she was calling out requests and they did their best, even when she asked for Taylor Swift. Ava approached Janna and between songs asked her about the keyboard and how she learned to play.

"I was six when I started taking piano lessons," Janna said.

"Did you take lessons for singing too?"

"Oh yeah, but that wasn't until I was older. I did choir in high school, but that teaches you to blend with everyone else. I wanted to stand out." Janna gave Ava a wink. "Do you like to sing?"

Ava nodded. "Mmhmm, but I don't do it for people. Like, I'm not in choir or anything."

"You know, I teach people to sing now. If I play a note on this keyboard, do you think you could try to match it?"

Ava gave a slow nod and Janna struck a key.

Dev wandered in to ask for a snack, and saw Ava standing next to Janna's keyboard. He asked Jack if he could try the drums.

Although neither child was interested in Mack's guitar, he was happy to see his kids experiencing something new. He wasn't sure Melissa would enjoy the learning curve on drums, but they did agree it was important to encourage their children's interests. Maybe Jack had been right about needing to show the kids their dad had a varied life. It would give them more experiences and opportunities to learn what else they might want to do or try.

On the drive home, Mack asked, "What did you guys think?"

"You need to learn some new songs," said Ava. "But it was cool. Janna said she could give me lessons if I want to learn to do vocals." She gave 'vocals' the emphasis of a new word.

"If Ava gets to learn to sing, I want to learn drums!" Dev said.

Ava turned from the front passenger seat to face her brother. "It's vocals, not just singing."

"Whatever. I want to play the drums."

"Sounds like we have the makings of a family band," Mack said. "We can talk about arranging some lessons as long as your mom is okay with it."

Dev started playing an invisible drum set, banging his head around and kicking his feet into his sister's seat.

"Stop it!" Ava reached around to swat at his feet, but she barely grazed them.

Mack was pulled from his imagining of the family band to deal with the squabbling.

*

For a time, Mack's focus was on the Supreme Court case, but after a few weeks, the judgment came down and all Mack's confidence in the future of the firm was shattered.

Over doughnuts at their break table, Mack broke the bad news to Gloria and Antonia. He was forthright with them about the financial position this put Poyfair Law in. Having asked them to take this risk with him, he felt it was only fair to keep them apprised of the situation.

"Well, hell," said Gloria. "What now?"

"The Polson Reed winnings will take care of the loan, right?" Antonia asked.

"Ideally, yes."

"There's no guarantees yet," said Gloria.

Antonia looked to Mack. "That's true," he said. "We want to get between three and five million dollars total, which will give us somewhere between one million and one point five million for our fees."

Antonia glanced at Gloria. "That seems okay," she said.

"That seems kind of close," Gloria said. "Remember, it's a line of credit. I don't have to pay it off entirely with our winnings. I'll put some toward the loan and some will go back into the firm. It's not as bad as it sounds. We have this case won, it's just a matter of how much we've won. We're going to ask for as much as we reasonably can so that after they reduce the penalties, we'll still get paid enough."

"Reduce the penalties?" Antonia asked.

"They almost always reduce the penalties," said Gloria. "Remember who our judge is for this. Those penalties might end up scraping the bottom of the barrel."

"That's why we start the negotiations at top dollar. Everything will work out okay." Mack reached for a doughnut, a little too intentional about the casual nature of the meeting. "The payday is coming. Let's just stay on top of anything that comes in regarding the Polson Reed case. What else do we have lined up?"

They ran through a few potential cases that had come in and then called an end to the meeting.

The next day, another blow arrived with a motion from Norris's firm.

"Defendant's Brief to Limit the Timeframe for Liability Period," Mack read under his breath. Norris's warning came back to Mack. "Antonia," he called out. "Set up a meeting for me with Aubrey Vassos, please? Gloria, I'm going to forward you a copy of this motion by the Humbert Lewis firm."

"What's up now?"

"They're asking to lower the liability period. We had them at eight years, but they're asking for a reduction to three."

"Based on what?" asked Gloria.

"A case between a driver and the grocery store chain he drove for. They're saying that the Erickson vs. Pennybasket case established the law that there must be separate compensation for non-driving time.

This case only happened three years ago, so they're saying we only have three years to claim on."

Gloria went silent as she read the motion and Antonia dialed Aubrey's number. As they went about their work, Mack imagined a match lighting his future on fire.

Chapter 18

"So what we're looking at here, Ms. Vassos, is the potential monetary difference if they win their argument for a limited timeframe," Mack told her when they met again at her office.

Aubrey started to pull up something on her computer, but Mack cut her off. "No actual reports, please. A physical or digital representation would obligate me to show it to the defense. While I trust your calculations completely, if there were any small error that you later correct, they would have ammunition to cast doubt."

Aubrey nodded. "I understand. You do, however, still have the original calculations, correct? The ones that included pre-shift, post-shift, rest breaks, and meal breaks?"

"That's correct."

"During the course of the case, I believe things were whittled down to just the rest breaks, yes?"

"Yes," Mack said. "At this point, they've entered a brief that claims the requirement for separate compensation wasn't law until three years ago, so they want to take six years out of our claim. I'm here because I want to know what that would do to our numbers. We're looking into their brief and the supposed evidence they have to back it up, but we want to know what we're facing if the judge agrees with them, and we're left with no recourse."

Aubrey nodded again. "Of course. I'm just going to pull up our original report that was submitted in the course of the trial." She clicked around on her computer and opened the report. Mack couldn't see the screen from this side of the desk and that was perfectly all right with him. "Why don't you head down the hall to the staff breakroom and get yourself a cup of coffee?" she suggested. "I'll run through the proposed numbers."

Mack rose and did as she suggested. He took his time and sipped coffee for a few minutes at one of the break tables while checking emails on his phone. Nothing new had come through, but he reread the one from Humbert Lewis that contained the brief.

This case would either make him or break him as an independent firm; he supposed the knowledge of what it represented for him was what made it so difficult. Finally, after his coffee was finished, Mack made his way back to Aubrey's office. He knocked gently on her door to announce his presence and she welcomed him in.

"It's not terribly complicated math once we removed everything but the rest breaks," she said as Mack resumed his chair across from her. "When it came to rest breaks, we were originally looking at three point six million dollars for nine years. With a two-thirds reduction of the timeframe, you're going to see more like a one point three-million-dollar total settlement."

Mack didn't need the formulas or a calculator to tell him that with the reduction, his attorney's fees would come in at a whopping four hundred thousand dollars. It wasn't nearly enough to start running the law firm on cash instead of credit. His expression must have shown his concern.

"Why don't we go grab something stronger than a coffee?" Aubrey suggested. "You look like you could use some liquid optimism."

Mack didn't even hesitate to take her up on the offer. It was late Friday afternoon anyway and he had been planning to head straight home from his meeting with Aubrey. The kids were with Melissa this weekend and Gloria and Antonia had both been granted early departure from the office.

Aubrey grabbed her jacket and purse and locked up her office behind them. "There's a bar just down the street," she said. "It's pretty popular with the college kids, but they don't usually fill it up until eleven. We're still within the civilized hours."

"Lead the way," Mack said.

At four-thirty in the afternoon, the bar only held a few post-work people and some barflies. They took a booth and ordered beers. "I'm sorry the numbers weren't more in your favor," Aubrey said.

Mack shrugged. "I knew it wasn't going to be good news. It was obviously going to be lower. When I took on this case, I thought we were looking at one hell of a payday. One that would set Poyfair Law on its feet. We're running on credit right now. Coming off the win at trial, I thought we were golden. Then a Supreme Court case I was in on fell apart, and this bullshit motion over the timeframe came in."

"One point two million isn't nothing," she offered.

"No, but my portion of it won't be what we need. Besides, their side is going to pick apart each plaintiff's work history to wheedle that number down as low as they can. I know you had vacation days accounted for in our original calculations, but they're going to look for sick days and late clock-ins...They're going to find everything they can. You're on our side, so naturally, your numbers are going to come out as much in our favor as they can. Their numbers will be a different, much more painful story." Mack took a healthy swallow from his beer.

"Of course," she said. "I hadn't thought of that." She sipped her own beer.

"The worst part is telling the members of the class."

Aubrey cocked her head.

"We've got six hundred and sixty-five drivers on this. Many of them are passive plaintiffs. They're just members of the class. They weren't asked to do depositions, they weren't questioned. All they had to do was not sign something saying they opted out. If all they get in the end is twenty bucks, that's not a huge deal to them, but for the drivers who brought this up, for the ones who lost their jobs in the course of it, the ones who've taken days off and sacrificed time to be there for meetings and the trial...a hundred bucks is not going to make all that seem worth it in the end."

"I see what you mean," she said. "Even with my 'plaintiff-friendly' number, they're only looking at a little over a thousand dollars each."

The last couple weeks had seemed like bad news stacking up and Mack was starting to worry about it turning around. They were still on the battlefield and Mack had to keep fighting, but on a Friday night, with a beer in front of him and pleasant company, he was ready to just forget the war for a while. "Let's talk about something else," Mack said. He looked at his watch. "It's now five o'clock, so technically, it's the weekend and there's no more work until Monday."

She narrowed her eyes. "Why don't I believe that you leave work at work at five?"

"It's true that during the week, I do bring a lot of work home with me. Especially when my kids are with their mom. There isn't much else to do. But I think I need a real weekend to wipe the slate clean before going back into the trenches on Monday. It's going to be another fight and I need a reprieve."

"Mmhmm. Well, I'm a professor, so sometimes, I have homework."

"Tell your students your dog ate it."

Aubrey laughed. "I've been tempted a time or two to leave it at her level and see if she would just get me out of it, but she's not a terribly destructive dog. Perhaps I shouldn't have made the mistake of training her so well when she was a puppy."

"What's your dog's name?"

"Harper. She's a border collie."

"I noticed her in your photos. Don't border collies usually need a job or a lot of exercise?"

"She's getting on in years now," Aubrey said, "but she gets a good run in the morning with me before work and a walk in the evenings. We're not terribly far from the beach so I take her out there on the weekends and she has a great time chasing birds. Tries to herd them, which is endlessly frustrating for her but gives her a great workout."

"I bet."

"Do you have any pets?" she asked.

"No. Dev, my son, was on about wanting a cat and Ava, my daughter, has asked for a puppy every Christmas since she was seven. But when Melissa and I separated, a pet just seemed like too much to add to the mix."

"I think you should consider getting them a pet, or rather, a pet for yourself. Something else to take care of on the weekends when you don't have your kids. They enrich your life, you know."

Mack laughed. "A friend of mine has been on my case for a couple months about needing to live a more fulfilling life. Of course, he has other ideas about what that entails, and there's some selfish motivation on his part."

"Oh yeah?" Aubrey ordered them a second round.

"Jack and I were in a band with some other friends back in college, and now his current band needs a substitute lead guitar for a while. He's been after me to fill in."

"The lawyer is a lead guitarist?" She raised an eyebrow. "I have to say, my image of lawyers came primarily from movies and TV before meeting you, and I guess I never imagined any of you having such fascinating alter egos."

"Anyone who knew me in my teen years probably would say that the lawyer persona is the alter ego. I started off college studying music."

"Really? Not to brag or anything, but I played the French horn in high school."

"You want to join Jack's band?" Mack asked.

"I stopped playing in college, but I did do a minor in music theory. There's a surprising number of math nerds with an overlap in music."

"Probably has something to do with all the counting," Mack said.

Aubrey went on to tell him about a project she'd done in college that overlaid the golden ratio with various music styles and songs. Math had never seemed terribly creative to Mack, but when Aubrey spoke about it in conjunction with his own passion, it seemed a lot more vibrant.

Hours later, they had gone through four rounds of beer and a few plates of food. Aubrey said she needed to get home to give Harper her supper. As they parted, Aubrey said, "Hey Mack, feel free to call me whenever you need some numbers crunched, but maybe give me a call for the hell of it now and then too." She gave him her personal number.

"I'll do that."

*

Monday morning, Mack was ready to put his armor back on. The set of his shoulders told Gloria and Antonia that he was ready for the war again.

"I know we thought we were on the homestretch," Mack began. "I know we were all set to just lock this case up and collect, but now we have this curveball to deal with. When I talked to Aubrey on Friday, she gave me some numbers that, quite frankly, just won't make any of us happy, let alone our clients. So, what we're going to do is tear apart this motion piece by piece until there's nothing standing, and then we can put our own numbers back on the board."

Gloria spread out the brief in front of her. "Their primary argument is that there was no ruling before

Erickson vs. Pennybasket regarding the requirement of separate compensation," she said.

"Okay," Mack said, "and what have you gathered on that case so far?"

She moved to a different set of notes. "Mr. Erickson was a driver for the Pennybasket grocery store chain. He sued them for rest break compensation and Pennybasket claimed the base rate already compensated for the rest breaks. It came down through the Court of Appeals that there needed to be separate compensation for the rest breaks. Pennybasket was appealing because they were certain their method of compensation was legal. That's part of Polson Reed's argument here. That because a huge chain like Pennybasket thought it was right, they appealed it all the way to the Supreme Court, where they lost. A chain like that would know what it's doing, so basically, Polson Reed's attorneys are now saying that combined compensation wasn't illegal until the ruling in Erickson vs. Pennybasket."

"So they're claiming there were no other rulings out there that supported the legality of separate compensation?"

"That's what it sounds like."

"Even though it wasn't a published ruling and it was at a district court level, the Ecklehurst case we did was on the same issue. That was, what, eleven years ago?"

"Around that, yes," Gloria confirmed.

"We went against Polson Reed under statute 226.2. That's not really a new statute. It codified Erickson vs. Pennybasket. Let me see those pages."

Gloria handed over the file with the Erickson vs. Pennybasket information in it. Mack started skimming through it and his eyes caught on the word 'Ecklehurst.' "There," he said. "This Erickson case referenced our suit against Ecklehurst. Ecklehurst Trucking used similar arguments against our clients and the judge dismissed them."

Mack scratched at the back of his neck.

"Do you have the trial transcripts handy?" Gloria asked Antonia.

"Sorry, I've gotten a little lost in all of this. Which trial do you want?"

"Polson Reed."

"Oh, yes." Antonia made some keystrokes and pulled up the searchable PDF. "What material are we looking for?"

"There were a few who claimed that rest breaks were paid through the route pay, that route pay was separate compensation," Gloria said. "If that's what they believed, then they knew about the legal requirement for separate compensation well before Erickson vs. Pennybasket. They said it was part of the compensation plan. Now, they're claiming they had no knowledge of this requirement prior to Erickson vs. Pennybasket. It seems to me, their own witnesses in the course of the trial absolutely bury their new claims."

"Can you find some of those passages in the transcript and highlight them? We need to put these disputes together into a brief and submit it," Mack said. He didn't want to say it out loud because the last time he was feeling confident had been right before everything fell apart. Still, this seemed promising. Maybe they could win this battle too.

Chapter 19

A full month later, Gloria and Mack were at a hearing set for discussing the timeframe of liability for Polson Reed. The defense trouped in with six lawyers, including both Aaron Norris and Harry Clark. After two hours of presentations and motions by every lawyer in the room, Judge Keats announced that he'd be taking it all under submission.

Every time Mack was stuck waiting for the next answer or the next hearing, there was a strange switching between emotions. One moment he would feel antsy and the next he would be relieved in the knowledge that there was nothing more he could do. As they were headed out of the courthouse, Harry Clark strode alongside Mack and said, "I think we should get a drink."

Mack agreed and they headed to a home-cooking restaurant a few blocks away. Harry ordered a beer so dark it looked black. Mack stuck to his usual light beer.

"You got kids?" Harry asked.

"Two," Mack said. "A boy and a girl. My daughter is the oldest."

"I got a son in college. He's on a soccer team there."

"My daughter plays soccer," Mack said. "She loves to run."

"It's a good sport for that," Harry said. "I was a basketball man, myself."

"Oh yeah? I played that a little too, in high school. Dev, my son, has been getting into it. I grew up in Texas, so, naturally, I was raised on football. Wasn't really my sport though."

"What brought you to California?"

"I was studying music. California was the place to be for that. I made the switch to law when I needed a more practical income, but by then, California was where my life was."

"Musician turned lawyer. Huh. We all take different paths, I guess."

The conversation went on from there. It wasn't clear to Mack what Harry's goal was in this impromptu meeting, but near the end of the fourth round of beers, he got to it.

"This case has been a hell of a trip," Harry said. "I think it might be time for us to go into mediation."

Mack managed not to choke on his beer. After the fight these guys had put up over every single thing, he had not expected this to come up. He scratched the back of his neck.

Harry Clark filled the silence with a prompt. "What do you think?"

Mack turned it over in his head for just a minute. "I'm going to have to say no, Harry. We're going to wait for the ruling. I appreciate this, though."

Harry nodded once. "Well, thanks for hearing me out. It was good to get to know you."

His gracious acceptance of Mack's refusal gave Mack an appreciation for the guy. Sometimes it was hard to see opposing counsel as anything other than the enemy, but Harry Clark was a good guy. They finished their beers and shook hands.

*

"What did Harry Clark want?" Gloria asked when Mack arrived at the office the next day.

"Let me get to my desk first, would you?" he replied. She trailed him all the way there and as soon as he sat down, she asked again.

"He offered mediation," Mack said.

She stared at him.

"I said no."

"Thank God," she said, throwing her hands up.

"Isn't that kind of a risk?" Antonia asked from her own desk. "What if Judge Keats agrees with their motion limiting the liability?"

"We'll deal with that if we need to, but if we went into mediation now—"

"We'd end up on the short end anyway," Gloria interrupted Mack. "We've only got one point three million dollars pending here. Accepting that in mediation would be screwing ourselves."

"Couldn't you negotiate for more? Isn't that what mediation is for?" Antonia asked.

"Sure, but if the judge agrees to the whole liability term, that's a much larger number. If we mediate, we're only going to end up in the middle of those two somewhere," Mack said.

Antonia bit her lip. "It seems like we're betting on Judge Keats rejecting their motion."

"We kind of are," said Mack. "Trust me, it's not an uncalculated risk, despite the four beers."

Antonia flicked her eyebrows up for a second, but said nothing more.

"It's the right call," said Gloria. "They kept swinging, so why should we sit down at a table with them now."

Mack appreciated her support, though he didn't have the same reasoning behind it as she. It would be another wait for an email declaring Judge Keats's ruling. Mack hoped it wouldn't be too long.

*

Jack called later that week and convinced Mack to rehearse with Porsche that night. "It's not a commitment to play with us," he said. "We just need someone to fill in for rehearsal for a bit."

"I thought you said just tonight?" Mack asked.

"Tonight, maybe Saturday too, if you can."

"Why do I feel like I'm just going to wake up one day a part of this band without ever having formally agreed to do it?"

"It's not a show, dude. Just rehearsal. C'mon."

Mack agreed and that night in Jack's basement, he was formally introduced to the members of Porsche.

"Emma is on bass and Declan does keyboards for us. You know Frank. Amalia is usually our lead guitar, but of course, you're filling in for her. This is Mack," Jack said to the assembled band.

Mack shook hands with the two members he didn't know and then Jack gave him a set list for them to rehearse. He surprised himself with how easy it was to keep up with the others. Since retrieving his guitar from the old house, Mack had been strumming a little almost every night, playing requests for his kids and fiddling around on it nights he was alone. The callouses of his band days had returned and did a good job protecting his fingers for the three-hour rehearsal.

Emma and Declan had families waiting for them and headed out immediately after the instruments were put to rest. Jack invited Frank and Mack to hang for a beer, to which they both agreed.

"You really held it together," Jack said to Mack as they found their places at his kitchen table.

"I guess even a little practice now and then refreshed my skills enough," Mack said.

"So you're in?" Frank asked.

"I did not say that," Mack protested.

"I don't understand why you're still saying no," Jack said. "You've had your law firm open for over a year now and you've been divorced just as long. You've got the kid thing and work. It's time to add something else."

"Because I don't live a fulfilling life?" he asked.

"Exactly."

"I've added dating."

"Those drinks with the opposing counsel happened months ago," Jack said.

"I'm talking about the mathematics professor. We went out after our meeting a month ago."

"A month ago?"

"Yeah."

"Nothing since then?"

"She said to give her a call."

"And you didn't?" Frank asked.

"She is an expert for the trucking case. Technically, the case is not over yet. I'm not sure we should go on a date while it's still in progress."

"The verdict is in," Jack said.

"But the numbers are still being debated and she works on the numbers, so what if I have to call her back in on something?"

"Did you tell her any of that?" Frank asked.

"She knows this stuff. She's a professional."

"Not in law, you idiot," Jack said. "Call her. Tell her you want to set up a date after the case is done."

"Yeah, fine," Mack said. "We've been emailing, so it's not like I shut it down."

"You're using this case as an excuse for a lot of things. There's always going to be a case, Mack. At least, if you are any good at your job."

"I get it, okay. I'll call her."

"I was referring to the band," Jack said. "But at least you're going to do that."

"Look," said Frank, "Julia said that she thinks your self-confidence really plummeted amid the divorce. Since then, she says, you take every single hit a little harder than you need to and every win a little lighter than you should."

Mack frowned. "Your wife is psychoanalyzing me in her spare time?"

"She psychoanalyzes everyone. Do you know how many times she pauses a movie to explain to me what psychological disorders are affecting the storyline? A two-hour movie takes three days to get through, not just because we have three kids."

"He's got three kids, a wife, a full-time day job, and he manages to find time for the band. Stop making excuses, man. Your law firm is doing fine and your kids are doing great and your guitar skills are up to par. It's time to move forward with something new. Something that's all for you."

"Starting to sound like it's all for you. Don't you have a guitarist who's coming back in a few weeks?" asked Mack.

Jack and Frank looked at each other. "The truth is, her husband got a promotion and they're heading across the country. We need someone permanent," Frank admitted.

"Haven't you auditioned anyone?" Mack asked.

"Sure, but they all sucked. Most of them were teenage kids who can't play worth a damn."

"Plus, they think lead guitar means they're in charge of the band," Frank said.

"Who did you have fill in for those gigs?"

"This guy, Arlo. He's already in a band. He was just helping us out."

"If you don't want to do it for yourself, do it for us," Frank said. "I can't take any more wiseass kids."

Mack drained the last of his beer. "I'll think on it. I'll practice with you for a week and if things still go smoothly and the case starts resolving, then we'll revisit it."

Jack and Frank took that as a firm yes and started laying out the schedule for the band over the next three months.

"Maybe we should kick Emma and Declan out and get the whole crew back," Frank joked.

"We're not reliving glory days," Jack said. "We're helping Mack here move forward." He clapped a hand on Mack's shoulder.

"Yeah, yeah, forward is the only way you can move," he said.

*

One week later the email came through with the ruling on the liability period. Mack read through it and held it up like a champion. "We got it," he said. "We got the whole class and the whole nine years."

Chapter 20

Hours after the ruling came through, Harry Clark called Mack and suggested mediation again. This time, Mack said yes. They agreed on a timeframe for the mediation and Mack suggested a judge who had recently retired. Harry agreed, so Mack contacted Judge George Adams to see if he was willing to oversee the mediation.

After setting up the mediation for three weeks from that day, Mack brought Gloria and Antonia up to speed.

"Why are we doing mediation now?" Antonia asked.

"We've got more to work with. Gloria, we need to file a motion with the court to enter final judgment."

"What are you up to?" Gloria asked.

"It's time to get this done. We need to put the pressure on. The mediation is set for three weeks from now and I want a hearing on this motion one week after that. That will put them on notice to settle this thing in mediation."

"Okay. What are the final numbers? Do I need to get in touch with Aubrey?" Her expression gave nothing away.

"That shouldn't be necessary," Mack said. "We have all her original calculations on record. The court will have to award class-wide damages and the attorney's fees. We need the original three point six million dollars for rest breaks, and then we want the interest too. I think she had that for us in the report, right? You may need to get in touch with her on the waiting time penalties to add those in. Then we have attorney's fees on top of that."

They scrambled to get the motion in as quickly as possible and after it was registered, there was another call from Harry Clark. "We're going into mediation, aren't we?" Harry asked. "Or did I miss something?"

"We're going into mediation," Mack confirmed.

"Then what the hell is this motion you've filed for final judgment?"

"The violations Polson Reed committed were intentional. I'm not looking to drag this on for another five years. If you want to, we're in it, but this is how it's going to go. We're looking to sew this up."

"You certainly are. Judge Adams wants our mediation briefs in two weeks. Was that not tight enough for you?"

"It is. I just want to make sure this mediation reaches a resolution in a timely manner."

"Do it your way then." Harry Clark hung up.

Gloria was working on the mediation brief while Mack and Antonia started putting together the exhibits for the mediation judge. Antonia was also making calls to the various drivers to set up another meeting. They needed to be updated and prepared for what mediation might entail for them.

*

Mack called the meeting to order with the drivers. "Here's where we're at. We've got our victory in the court." He paused for the celebration. "Now we're working out what Polson Reed will be paying you guys in terms of missed pay, interest, and fees. We're going to enter mediation with them and to put the pressure on, we've submitted a motion for final judgment. The mediation hearing is in a week and a half. A week after that is the final judgment. There's a small window for us to work things out with the other side.

"The judge we have for mediation has a specific way he likes to do things. Basically, we send over a number and then the defense gets to respond. Then we send over a second number. They respond. Then a third number. After that, he sees us in mediation. We've gone through the numbers exchange already and they stonewalled us, so we are definitely going to mediation with Judge Adams." Mack's final number had been no different from his second because Polson Reed's team had offered a single, unreasonably low, sum and had refused to move from it even a single cent.

"Mediation will be different than the trial. For the trial, you were able to show up on the days you were needed. Mediation takes all day and you all need to be there for the whole thing. Everyone must dress up. We're going to be asking for a lot of money and you've got to look like you understand the gravity of the dollar amount."

"What if we can't be there?" Patrick Yost asked. "What if we have a route that day and they won't let us out of it for the mediation?"

"We've got a letter here that can be signed to give your settlement authority to the designated reps. It gives them the authority to resolve the complaint on your behalf. Basically, you're saying you trust the representatives who can be there in person to reach a settlement for you. However, I encourage all of you to do your damnedest to be physically present at the mediation. It's important that we show how serious this is."

After resolving any further questions, Mack called the meeting to a close, but a few lingered after for coffee. Barry Beady was one of them.

"Hey, Mack," he said. "I heard about something going on with the American Truckers Association. Polson Reed is a part of that, and I got in on a mailing list for drivers about stuff going on with their lobby. Anyway, the ATA is petitioning against the state law in California. Wilcom, this senator, he's backing it. As far as I can tell, their petition says if a trucking company is going over state lines, they don't have to follow California's pay laws or something like that."

Mack held his composure. "Did you happen to bring that material with you? Or could you get it to my office?"

"Sure, sure thing. I'll email it to you when I get home." Barry paused. "The thing is...will this be able to affect our case? If it passes, I mean? We already won, right? Now, they're just talking numbers, but does that mean it's done or...?"

"I can't say anything for certain without having a look at it," Mack said. "Don't get too worried about it though, kid. We've got Polson Reed pinned to a timeclock as best we can, and I won't let this drag out any longer. Just send me what you have on that amendment and I'll take a look."

Mack said good-bye to the lingering truckers and then shared with Gloria and Antonia the information Barry had provided.

"We need to look into it and see how much pressure this puts on us," Mack said. He hadn't wanted to worry Barry or any of the other truckers over it, but this new information took up residence in his mind as a potential issue. "I have Barry sending me what he's got on it, but Antonia, I want you doing some independent research on where this amendment is at and what it really says."

She wrote down the senator's name and they agreed to start fresh on it tomorrow morning. While Mack had Harry Clark, Aaron Norris, and all the others at Polson Reed up against the ropes between mediation and final judgment, this business in Congress could threaten to undo everything. Getting this done quickly had never mattered more than it did now. There never seemed to be a moment where this case let him breathe for longer than a minute. Every time he turned around, Mack found a new pressure or problem or brief falling from the sky. It was starting to feel like Isaiah entering his office that first day was the beginning of a long test to see if he really could run his own law firm.

*

The next afternoon, Antonia presented Mack with everything she had found on the ATA petition and Senator Wilcom. Mack reviewed it carefully. Wilcom was obviously very sympathetic to the trucking industry, and his proposed amendment spoke to that. It would create a new law that would preempt California state law when it came to wage-an-hour laws. Despite having a win in court with a jury, until the final judgment was entered, it was still open to this potential new law. In short, if the Wilcom amendment went through before the final judgment or the settlement was resolved, Mack, his firm, and the Polson Reed drivers would be screwed.

Mack ran his hand through his hair. The thinness couldn't be ignored, nor could the strands caught between his fingers after the aggravated gesture. He could not afford to lose out entirely on this case. Even the measly one point three million dollars would give him a wobbly standing to take on another large case. But they had fought so hard to get to this point where there would absolutely be money on the table—significant money. It wasn't enough to do battle inside the confines of the case, now he had to do it while racing Congress and Senator Wilcom. It can take months to get a settlement agreement finalized with all the details. Even if Mack could resolve things at mediation, there was still time for this amendment to undo everything.

It was nearly six o'clock. Mack stood up from his desk and gathered his things. As he went past Gloria's desk, he said, "I've got to go pick up my kids, but this Wilcom amendment…" He ran his hand through his hair again. "It could be a problem for us if it goes through. Frankly, it could tear the floor right out from under our case and we'd be left with nothing. Not one damn dime."

"Shit," Gloria said. "How is it looking in terms of going through?"

"It's no slam dunk, but we can't rule it out. The good news is Congress is always slow, but we've got to take this mediation seriously and we've got to get a settlement out of it as quickly as possible. We have to be on their asses about it."

"Senate elections are coming up too," she said. "If this Wilcom gets voted out, we could be free and clear."

"Let's not go betting on elections to go our way. We've had to fight for every little thing in this case. Counting on luck seems downright foolish now."

"Of course," said Gloria. "Wouldn't hurt to throw a donation into his opponent's campaign though, right?"

Mack gave her a wan smile. "Certainly couldn't." All he could think as he walked out the door was how he really couldn't afford to be contributing to political campaigns right now.

*

"Why don't you come in and join us?" Melissa offered when she answered the door. "We were just sitting down to eat."

Mack accepted the invitation and followed her back to the dining room table.

"Dev, why don't you grab a place setting for your father," she said.

Dev hopped up from his chair and grabbed the various items and laid them out in front of the chair across from Melissa's—Mack's old place, where he had eaten nearly every night. He sat and dishes clinked as they were passed around and baked spaghetti was scooped onto plates. There was silence for a while as Dev shoveled food into his mouth and Ava observed her parents over her slow bites.

Finally, Melissa cleared her throat. "How is the new firm going?" she asked.

Mack presumed that she had burned through all the school talk with the kids already and was trying to be polite. It had been over a year now. They needed to be able to have friendly conversations. This was just such a bad time and place for that question.

"It's going fairly well," he said. "We're moving into mediation for that class-action trucking case." He searched for another direction in conversation and his eyes landed on Ava. "The kids were asking about music lessons. Do you remember Janna, from my old college band?"

Melissa nodded.

"The kids were with me over at Jack's house and she was showing Ava some vocal techniques. She offered to give her lessons if we're okay with it."

"Ava mentioned singing with her. I didn't know Janna had offered to teach her."

"Don't forget me!" Dev said. "I want to learn drums!"

Melissa met Mack's eyes for a second and then, realizing that silent communication didn't work so well anymore after all the time apart, said, "That seems like a very loud instrument to learn…"

"We can get him a set at my place," Mack offered. "He could practice there."

"Won't he need to practice when he's staying here too?" Melissa asked. "They could go in the second car stall in the garage, I suppose."

Mack cleared his throat. "I guess we're going to need two sets if we don't want to be transporting them all the time."

"They are kind of a bulky instrument, aren't they?" Melissa said.

"And expensive," Mack said.

Ava was bouncing her eyes between them as they spoke. "Maybe Dev could learn something smaller. He could take voice lessons like me," she said.

Dev looked alarmed at this, but Mack hastened to reassure him. "We want you to learn whatever instrument you want. We're just working out the logistics. Right, Mel?"

Melissa blinked and stayed silent for a beat. Then she looked at Dev. "Of course. You should learn whatever you want. We'll figure out the details." She waved a hand and then changed the subject to prompt Dev and Ava to tell Mack about their day at school.

After Mack got the kids home and Dev settled in with a video game for an hour before bed, Ava approached Mack who was sitting at the dining table with his guitar.

"Dad," she whispered, glancing to where Dev sat in the living room. "It's not a big deal if the lessons are too complicated. I don't really need to learn to do vocals and Dev doesn't need to learn the drums."

"What are you talking about?" Mack rested his guitar in his lap. "Do you want to learn to sing like a professional?"

"Well, yeah, but it sounds like it'll be kind of difficult with you and Mom living in different places. I don't want it to make you guys mad at each other or anything."

"You and your brother wanting to pursue new things isn't going to make your mother and me fight. We want you to learn everything you want to learn. It won't be complicated. We just need to decide whether transporting the drums makes more sense than buying two sets. It's not a problem, honey." Mack searched her face. "You understand that we weren't disagreeing, right? We were just talking about how to make this happen for you guys."

"Are you sure? It sounded like you might disagree on which thing to do and then that might be a fight."

"Ava, I promise you, this isn't the kind of thing we would fight about. When it comes to you kids, it's incredibly easy for us to get along and figure things out. We agree that we want you guys to be happy and to choose your own way in life, so we're always going to encourage that."

"Okay," Ava said.

"Besides, I really think a family band might be a good idea," he said, trying to lighten her mood. "We can play songs on YouTube and get discovered!" he said.

Ava laughed. "That only happened to, like, one person."

"It could happen again." He smiled and started strumming a song that Ava knew very well. He started mixing up lyrics until she interrupted him and started singing the right ones. Mack loved to hear her sing, her voice still childlike and full of air. When she'd started this conversation, she seemed burdened, but her singing soon brought her to dancing and then she was wrapped in pure joy.

Chapter 21

"*W*hy are you reading about judo?" Gloria asked as she and Mack waited in the courthouse for their mediation timeslot.

"Judge Adams is a judo competitor," Mack said, thumbing through the magazine he had brought.

"I thought he was retired," Gloria said.

"He is. He's also in his sixties, but he still competes."

"Wow." Gloria whistled.

"Figured it couldn't hurt to build some rapport with him and try to work it into our strategy."

Soon after, the doors were unlocked and the drivers began arriving. Every single one of the class representatives had found a way to make it in person.

Judge Adams began the mediation conversationally. "Litigation has a lot in common with judo," he said.

Mack made brief eye contact with Gloria. "Judo is the art of using your opponent's weight against them. I've looked over your briefs and the case history and it seems like you have been slinging each other all over the place throughout this. I hope we can agree that we are here to reach an agreement today. It's been determined that Polson Reed Trucking was in the wrong and now we need to sort out the money. I want good faith proposals and serious investment in this process today."

Mack had a feeling that the judge was addressing this due to the defense's poor showing in the initial offer. After both sides affirmed that they were hoping to come out of this with a settlement, the mediation began.

Mack presented his new strategy to Judge Adams. "You can see from the progression of the case that this has been a piranha-like attack. We came at them from so many angles and in every way we could. They responded by trying to sue us and putting up sanctions against us. The defense has been very aggressive. We had the other case against them too, regarding pre-shift and post-shift time. We've been attacking on every front, but I want to take this piranha attack—which few people survive—and change it to a shark attack. It hurts, but most people survive shark attacks.

We're not here to ruin Polson Reed. We're here to make sure the drivers are compensated, and the employer remembers to follow the rules. I'm offering a one-time bite for Polson Reed. PAGA penalties, non-driving work time, pre-shift, post-shift, meal breaks, everything we've been coming at you with, we're going to tie it all up. We're going to settle all these labor problems."

Judge Adams nodded, smiling. "Okay. That sounds great. Let's review the particulars and then we'll get to numbers, shall we?"

Four hours into the mediation, after a lunch buffet, Judge Adams said, "Let's get to the numbers. Mr. Poyfair, what is it you're asking?"

"Thirteen million dollars."

The whole Polson Reed crew of lawyers and big shots huddled up for a good forty-five minutes and then came back with their counter offer. "Three million, three hundred, sixty-seven thousand dollars," Harry Clark stated.

Mack ignored the hubbub behind him among the drivers. They clearly noticed the discrepancy, but they didn't know what the early numbers had been. They didn't know that Polson Reed's first mediation submission had been zero dollars and their second a mere seventy-five thousand. The fact that they were willing to talk seven figures had Mack very pleased. Progress could be made today after all.

Mack's team discussed their next move.

"At least they're taking this seriously now," Gloria said.

"Judge Adams did ask for everyone to show that they were here in good faith," said Antonia.

"It's a good faith number, for sure," said Mack. "But we're not going to just take a number that shows they're willing to deal. Let's go eleven million. That's a significant decrease and will show that we're also here to reach an agreement, but it will also make it clear that we are willing to take this as far as necessary."

They agreed on the number and presented it. The other side went into an intense discussion where things were obviously getting heated, subdued though they were.

"We can take this to appeals," Harry Clark said to Mack. "We've been at this over a year, and we can keep going."

"I understand that," Mack said, "but we can appeal on the meal breaks and we can appeal on the other side, and this can keep going until it isn't eleven million anymore, but thirty-six million. Is that where you want to take this?"

Harry Clark waved a hand and went back to the rest of his team who were still discussing numbers.

Gloria raised her eyebrows at Mack for a second. "They might bet on us going bankrupt," she said.

"They might," said Mack, "but they don't want to spend the rest of their careers on this case."

"They could just hold out until that Wilcom amendment," she whispered. Mack didn't say anything to that. Gloria was seeing their side a little too clearly for Mack's taste right now. He wanted to keep the Wilcom amendment out of his mind.

After over an hour of deliberations, Harry Clark presented Polson Reed's new offer. "Four million."

Mack did his best to contain any physical sign of his irritation. He had come down two million dollars on his initial number and their response was to raise by less than seven hundred thousand? He exhaled in a highly controlled manner.

"That's not going to work for us," said Mack.

"That's what we're offering," Harry replied. Mack didn't believe for a second that Harry thought that was a fair way to play this, but Norris was over there too, and the Polson Reed execs were still insisting they'd done nothing wrong.

As the debate began with neither side shifting their offer, Judge Adams interrupted. "It's getting on to five o'clock here and we seem to have gotten stuck. Can I just borrow Mr. Poyfair for a minute in private?"

Mack followed Judge Adams into a smaller room across the hall where they sat down at a conference table.

"I understand that you're trying to get everything taken care of here and now, Mr. Poyfair. You've got eleven million out there and they've got four. What I'm wanting to know is where your attorney fees are at."

"I do expect my fees to be paid," Mack said. "They could do it separately, but they don't want to. We're at over two million in billable hours. I'm not going to let go of that. At four million…well, that doesn't really leave much. If this was early on, in the first months of this case, then we'd be on board with four, but at this stage…It's just unreasonable. I came down two million from the first ask and they've barely budged."

"I know it. I can see you all are getting stuck and this whole case has seen a lot of back and forth. At this point, I'm going to suggest a mediator's compromise."

A mediator's compromise would mean a number presented by the judge to each side that they could each refuse or agree to and neither would know what the other said unless both agreed.

"I need to find a number here between four and eleven. They've said they won't do a dollar over five. You've said you're not gonna go a drop below eight."

Mack did the math fast enough to know dead center between their limits was six-point-five.

"I think a mediator's compromise is the right way to go here. It's getting late and we're just going back and forth now." Mack scratched his neck. "You know something? My favorite number, kind of my lucky number, is seven. I was born on March seventh and Ava was born at seven-oh-seven in the morning. Dev was born on the seventh of July. It's a good number."

Judge Adams gave him a smile. "It's lucky in Vegas, too. Let's head back in there."

The room full of lawyers, paralegals, and clients had risen a little in volume during their absence, but Judge Adams quickly called the room to order.

"Since we're stalled out here, I'm going to make a mediator's proposal of seven million dollars. I'll take your private responses to that."

"Your Honor," Harry Clark said, "the fact of the matter is, there's a major stakeholder in Polson Reed who is not present here today. He has given us authorization for five million to settle a case. We need to discuss it with him before we can go over that."

"Very well," Judge Adams said. "It's seven million and that is open until noon tomorrow. All parties can consult with their respective people and must respond by tomorrow at noon."

With that, the mediation was left for the evening. Mack officially submitted an agreement to the seven million and the waiting game began again. Thankfully, there was a clock on it this time.

*

Janna was at the house with Mack's kids. It had worked out well that Janna wanted to do Ava's first lesson that night and was able to come early to be with the kids while Mack was still in mediation.

They were clearing away their supper dishes when Mack came in. "Please tell me there are leftovers," he said.

"We saved you a plate," Ava said, presenting it to him. Mack dropped his bag on the floor and welcomed the plate of warmish food. It was a simple stir fry with rice, and spicy enough that the smell made his mouth water and his nose tingle.

"What angels you are," he said, taking his seat at the table to consume his meal. "Did I miss the voice lesson?" he asked.

"We're going to start after the dishes are done," Ava said.

"I'll do the dishes when I'm done eating," Mack said. "You two give me some dinner music."

Ava didn't need to be convinced. Janna followed her to where Janna's travel keyboard was set up against the living room wall, next to the TV. She had brought along a couple of lesson books. "Let's start with what a scale is and the way to read notes."

Dev's new drums were in his room, waiting for the following night when Jack would come by to show Dev the basics. The lack of lessons did not stop Dev from testing out the set over the weekend, but Mack had had to put a strict limit on his "practicing" so that Ava could concentrate on her homework. Now, Dev was sitting at the table with Mack, watching Ava and Janna.

As Ava cooed out her first notes, matching them with the notes Janna had her strike on the keyboard, Mack snapped a photo with his phone and sent it to Melissa before he second-guessed himself too much. Back when the kids were small and they were still married, firsts were always captured and shared as much as possible. Their kids would continue to have many firsts and it wasn't fair to have them divided into his memories and Melissa's memories. They should still share these moments if only to share in the growth of the wonderful people they had brought into the world.

Melissa sent back a message soon after: *Thanks for sending that.*

"She's not even singing a song," Dev whispered to Mack.

"It takes time to learn," Mack told him. "You'll see when you start your lessons."

"At this rate, she'll be in college before we get to have a family band."

"You like the family band idea?" Mack asked.

"Yeah. You told Ava we could put videos on YouTube and be famous!"

"To be honest, we probably won't get famous, but it would be a good time and it would be a good way for your grandparents to get to see you guys playing."

"That's still pretty cool, I guess," Dev said. "Nobody else in my class has a YouTube channel."

Dev left the table then to go to his room. Mack finished eating and did the dishes, as promised, while Janna and Ava wrapped up their lesson.

"So just practice those until next week and we'll see how you're getting along then," Janna said. "Concentrate on your breathing though, okay? Practicing every day is the best way to really learn it. Especially practicing the day after the lesson, while it's still fresh in your memory."

"This was fun, Janna. Thanks," Ava said.

Janna entered the kitchen as Mack was emptying the dishwater, but Ava was still plucking away at the keyboard and singing.

"She did her homework already, right?" Mack asked.

"Yep. Right after school," Janna said. "I think she's going to stick with this. Her enthusiasm didn't wane at all, even when she was just practicing breathing. She's got music in her blood."

"At least I can give them that passion," he said.

"Frank said that you're in Porsche now," Janna said.

"Not really. Not a hundred percent." He dried his hands.

"Frank sounded pretty certain."

"I'm practicing with them. I haven't done a gig yet."

Janna nodded. "Frank says you're in, so my guess is, you'll be gigging soon."

"I keep telling them that I need to wrap up this case first."

"There will always be another case, Mack."

"That's what Jack said."

"It's true."

"Of course, but it won't always be this case. It won't always be the case that..." Mack broke off to ensure Ava was still engaged in her music, then he continued at a whisper. "It won't always be the case that decides if I still have a law firm."

Janna raised her black eyebrows. "It's that serious?"

"I've put everything I have into this. Tomorrow I'll know if the opposition has agreed to the mediator's proposal. After that, we'll either be going to final judgment next week or we'll need to get cracking on finalizing the settlement. We can't sustain this much longer without a cash influx and we definitely can't sustain it if this amendment goes through." Mack raked his hand through his hair, unconsciously, and then realized what he'd done and gripped the countertop with his hand instead.

"Amendment?"

"There's an amendment being sponsored by Senator Wilcom. It would basically chuck our whole case out the window, despite our victory in court. It would just...undo that. We'd be left with squat."

"That's..." Janna went to a whisper as well. "That's kind of terrifying, Mack."

"It's probably not as drastic as it feels," he said. "Congress is at least good at dragging their feet." He smiled and Janna laughed.

"Good luck with it," Janna said. "I've got get home, but I'll be back next week for Ava's next lesson. If that works for you?"

"Next week will be at her mom's. You remember the old place?"

"Oh, yeah, of course." Janna brushed past the awkwardness. Mack wondered if she would feel uncomfortable around Melissa, given that she was Mack's friend and had never spent significant time with Melissa. Just one more thing to navigate in the land of divorce.

Janna said her good-byes and headed out. Ava finally stopped practicing around nine when Mack told her she needed to go to bed. The kids had their good-night call with Melissa and they went to bed. Mack sat up watching the news for a while, lightly picking at his guitar in the dark living room with only the TV for light.

*

The next day, Judge Adams called Mack at 11:45 a.m.

"How's it going, Mr. Poyfair?" he asked.

"It's a pretty nice day. How are you doing?" Mack asked. The politeness required of him in law sometimes left him clenched.

"Not bad. I've got a judo competition coming up this weekend. I think I mentioned that to you yesterday?"

"Yes, you did," Mack confirmed.

"Right, well, that means I'm training pretty hard today and then I go light the rest of the week. I'm really looking forward to it. Some of my favorite opponents are coming and we always have a great time." The judge went on to detail the location and parameters of the competition and all Mack could think was, *Did they say yes or not?* He made all the appropriate interested sounds at the right times and tried to avoid asking questions. Finally, Judge Adams got to the point. "So," he said, "I had a chat with Harry Clark an hour or so ago and you've got a deal at seven million."

Mack stood up from his chair involuntarily. Gloria and Antonia both looked at him.

"That's great," Mack said to the judge. "Thank you so much for your help in this mediation."

"You're welcome. It wasn't a bad way to spend a day, all in all. I'm glad it worked out for you."

"Good luck at your tournament this weekend," Mack said.

"Thank you, Mr. Poyfair. You have a good day now."

They ended the call and Gloria and Antonia both approached Mack's desk. He didn't keep them waiting. "They agreed to seven million."

"Thank God," Gloria said.

"Wonderful!" Antonia said.

"Let's update the clients and get in touch with Harry Clark and Aaron Norris. This deal isn't done until it's on paper."

Chapter 22

Mack certainly wasn't going to mention to Harry Clark why he was anxious to get the settlement paperwork done, but he was pretty sure Harry was also well aware of Wilcom's amendment. Mack sent the thirty-page settlement agreement as soon as they could get it together, and now Harry Clark and all the others were dragging their feet. Mack called to check in a week after he first sent it for signatures. After pleasantries, he got right to it. "How are things going with getting that settlement agreement signed?"

"Everyone's got to look it over, you know, so it's taking some time," he said.

"When do you think you'll be ready with it?" Mack pressed.

"Hmm...let me see now. Norris's team is going over it right now. I suppose, maybe next week."

"All right then, Harry. I look forward to seeing it."

The week passed and nothing came, and Harry didn't volunteer any updates. Mack gave him a grace day and then called again. "What's the word on the settlement?"

"You know that stakeholder we mentioned at the mediation? Sato's his name. He's over in Japan and he's got a personal lawyer he wants to check it out."

Mack sucked his teeth. "When do you expect to hear back from him?"

"For sure by next week."

The week passed with silence. Mack sent Harry an email asking him to get the show on the road. Harry replied with more excuses every time Mack followed up: So-and-so was on a fishing trip. Sato's lawyer wanted another look, his kid was in a play and he couldn't talk now, etc. After five weeks, the lines of communication were virtually silent on Harry's end, with only his assistant responding to Mack in emails. It was clear to him they were trying to buy time. The approaching election meant that Wilcom was spending more time on that than his amendment, but his popularity had Mack convinced Wilcom would be reelected. With that reelection would come the full swing on the amendment. With the verbal agreement to the seven million dollars, the hearing for final judgment had been taken off the books. Mack was left holding nothing until that settlement got signed and approved by the court.

It was now mid-October, and Mack was considering contacting Harry again, just to keep the pressure up. That's when his cell phone rang and Aubrey's name came across the screen. He answered.

"So, I thought I told you to give me a call," Aubrey said, "but all you've done is text me. What would you say to a dinner date on Friday?"

Mack found the idea appealing. "Absolutely. Let's do it."

They set a time and place, then Aubrey said she'd let him get back to work and they ended the call.

This would be his first real date since the divorce. The first one planned and executed as a date. He had been avoiding calling Aubrey for a date. Despite the fun they'd had with the impromptu drinks, Mack had found himself hesitant of making anything official. But it was another step he would need to take eventually, and Aubrey was great company for it.

*

Mack had noticed the hair on his head thinning drastically over the last several months, but that night as he prepared for bed, his head started to tingle. He put a hand to it and a large clump of hair came out with no scratching or other disturbance of the follicles. "What the hell?" He looked at himself in the mirror, turning his head to get a view of where the hair came out. Jack had commented at the last band rehearsal that Father Time was obviously catching up with Mack. It was something he'd been working to accept, but this was entirely different. As he examined himself in the mirror, he realized his eyebrows were vanishing as well. There were wisps of dark hair where there had once been furry caterpillars.

Is this more than stress and old age? He took out his electric trimmer and contemplated taking what was left of his hair off his head. He went as far as turning it on before deciding it could wait until morning. He would check his head in the daylight and see if drastic measures were really needed.

The morning left him with little need for any sort of shaving. A lot of his hair had fallen out during the night and his morning shower took care of even more. The bald spot was spreading aggressively. He took stock of himself and realized, there was very little hair left on his body anywhere. He called Gloria to inform her that he would be working from home for a couple days.

He called his doctor and set an appointment for Friday morning, which was two days later. He contemplated canceling his date with Aubrey but decided to see how things went with Dr. Laghari first. Not that he expected to grow his hair back by eight the next night, but having answers might make it easier to see Aubrey with some confidence.

When he first told the doctor that he was there because he was losing his hair, Dr. Laghari chuckled. "We're all losing our hair, friend. That's part of aging."

"You don't understand. This bald patch that has nearly consumed my head started on Tuesday. Look my face. There's no stubble and I haven't shaved all week."

Dr. Laghari lowered the exam table so he could get a good look at Mack's head. "When did this start?"

"A few months ago I noticed the thinning hair on my head. I've been on a big case and so I figured stress and aging, but earlier this week, it just came out in wads. Honestly, there's hardly any hair left on me anywhere." Mack held out his arms for the doctor to see.

"I see that."

Dr. Laghari examined Mack a while longer and then said, "I want to do a scalp biopsy."

"What?"

"A scalp biopsy. I'll just cut away a little of your scalp."

"What are you testing for?"

"Frankly, I think it will merely be confirmation. This pattern of hair loss is typical of alopecia universalis."

"Alopecia?"

"Yes."

"What's the treatment?" Mack asked.

"It's an autoimmune disease. There's no known cause and there is currently no cure."

"Are you shitting me?" Mack couldn't help the turn of phrase. "So that's it, I'll be hairless for the rest of my life?"

"We'll do the biopsy to confirm. I can't say anything for certain, but sometimes it comes and goes. Autoimmune diseases can be like that, triggered or sort of dormant."

Mack sat in silence for several beats.

"Are you ready for the biopsy?" Dr. Laghari asked eventually.

"Yeah, okay," Mack said.

*

After his appointment, Mack went home and shaved his head. If he was still going on the date, he wasn't going to go with a patchy head. The lingering eyebrow wisps could stay if they could hold on until that evening. He figured he'd better go on the date now before his eyebrows were gone entirely. He wasn't sure how he'd feel going around without eyebrows, let alone going on a first date without them.

He met Aubrey outside O'Neill's Bar and Grill.

"New look," she said after saying hello.

"Yeah," he said, running a hand over his scalp. "It's not entirely by choice."

"Oh?" Her brow furrowed. "Is everything all right? You're not…sick, are you?"

Mack knew that a bald head usually signaled cancer to people, so he said, "No. The doctor thinks it's alopecia. I had a test this morning for confirmation."

"I'm sorry. You do seem to pull off the bald look as well as you did the full head of hair, though."

"Thank you," he said. His shoulders slid down from their tensed position and he gestured toward the door of the restaurant. "Shall we get some dinner?"

"Absolutely. This is one of my favorite places."

"Then you'll be able to tell me what to order," Mack said.

They passed another lovely evening together. Mack told her about the kids taking up instruments and she shared a little about her French horn days.

At the end of the meal, Mack walked her to her car. He was contemplating kissing her good-night when a breeze passed over his scalp and he remembered he was bald now. His confidence faltered, but Aubrey leaned toward him and initiated the kiss herself. She smoothed a hand over his head. "It's getting chillier in the evenings now. You're going to need a hat."

"I guess so, huh."

"I knit," she said.

"Can you knit me some eyebrows?"

She ran a hand over his smooth jaw. "I think you'll be just fine without them."

*

By the following Monday, every hair on his body was gone.

Chapter 23

*O*n Election Day, while everyone else was watching the presidential race, Mack had his eye on the senatorial race for California. He stayed up late into the night, watching the results come in. In the end, as a highly conservative, big-business president was voted in, the same type of man was voted out of the California senate. Mack toasted his colleagues the following morning with coffee.

"Wilcom lost," he said. "Without the man backing the amendment, the ATA has no one to press it on Congress. Polson Reed is going to have to get off their asses now and get this settlement done."

Gloria raised her dark roast with two sugars and Antonia her mochaccino.

"Thank the Lord we don't have that amendment hanging over us anymore. I felt like we were sitting on a chopping block," Gloria said.

"I'm going to give Harry a little time to get that settlement agreement to us on his own. In the meantime, let's get a motion for preliminary approval drafted so we can drop this thing on the court immediately after we receive it. If they're going to keep dragging their feet, we're going to have every step prepared for immediate submission. We won't be the ones holding this back."

"Of course," Gloria said.

They started work on the motion that day and by the time Harry Clark sent over the completed settlement agreement the following Monday, it was ready for filing. Mack immediately submitted it to Judge Keats and set up a hearing as quickly as he could for preliminary approval. Thanksgiving was approaching and after that, getting things done before the end of the year tended to get difficult.

Rather than a full hearing, the judge sent Mack an email:

> *I'm happy to see you guys want to settle this case. I've received all your documentation and you have preliminary approval. You can send*

out the notices to the class members. Work out
what your final billings are and what you want
for all the class representatives. I look forward to
getting this done.

Regards,
Judge Marcus Keats

His approval didn't surprise Mack at all. Judges almost always granted preliminary approval. It was the final approval that sometimes fell through, and on top of that, the judge could approve the settlement but deny the attorney's fees.

Mack shared the good news with his staff and asked Antonia to find the name of the notice company they had used in the past. Mack didn't mind spending the extra money, even if his fees weren't confirmed yet. Right now, timing mattered more to him than anything else. They needed class members to respond thirty days before the final approval hearing, so the hearing couldn't be set until the notices went out.

Mack had a lunch date with Aubrey that day and she asked how his day was over chicken salad sandwiches at a diner that had become their meeting spot during work days. "We have our preliminary approval and we're going to get notices out to the class members in the next couple days."

"That sounds great. You're coming into the final stretch, right?" she said.

"That's a fair assessment. Nothing in law is ever done until it's signed, sealed, and delivered though. We'll have to see how the class members respond. They can still opt out. Few ever do, but it can affect our approval, and there's no guarantee on my fees yet."

"I don't know how you can live with so many possibilities all the time. I would find that so stressful," Aubrey said. "I like the predictability of my work. The security of it."

"It's not like being a lawyer is necessarily inherently risky, but I wanted to have my own firm. The risks I'm facing are more like those any business owner would face when starting out. It takes time to reach stability, but it eventually comes. Even if the cases are sometimes lost or fall apart in the end, you start to find a balance as long as some things go right for you at the beginning."

"That makes sense. Why would a class member opt out? It's not like being in it costs them anything, right?"

"It doesn't, but some opt out so they have their right to sue independently on the issue for themselves. The notices give them the option to do nothing and be a part of the lawsuit settlement, opt out to keep their own right to legal action, or they can object to the settlement. We need their response thirty days before the final approval so the sooner these go out, the sooner we can set that hearing."

"What happens if they object to it?"

"We figure out why they object to it and see if it is an error. For example, the notices will say what the settlement is for and what amount they are likely to receive from that based on the time they have worked in the liability window. Someone might come forward and say that they actually worked more than what we recorded."

"Will you be needing my services again if someone raises that type of concern?" Aubrey asked.

"Actually, we hire a third-party administrator to figure those things out with the person directly. It can end up being a very one-on-one gig communicating with the class members who call in just to ask questions and to get these discrepancies sorted out." Mack waved a hand. "We're running out of lunch break here. Tell me about your morning."

"It's been a fairly good one. I was going to ask if you have plans for Thanksgiving next week," Aubrey said. "I usually have dinner with my parents, and I thought maybe you would want to come along. If you're free."

"I'm sorry, but I actually have the kids for Thanksgiving," said Mack. "We are going to my brother's place near San Diego."

"That's great that you get to have the kids," Aubrey said. "A few of my nieces and nephews will be at my parents' place too. I think kids make holidays much more fun."

"You have so many siblings, I'm not surprised you enjoy chaotic holidays."

Aubrey smiled. "It's true, while I like the order and structure of mathematics, it just doesn't feel like a holiday if the noise doesn't nearly blow the roof off." She looked at her watch. "I think we better call it. I'm already late getting back for office hours."

"Of course." Mack stood up. "I'll get the bill. You can take off."

"Thank you," Aubrey said, taking her jacket off the chair. "I'll talk to you later?"

"Looking forward to it." They parted with a kiss and on his way back to work, Mack wondered if he was supposed to have invited her to his family Thanksgiving. If he didn't have the kids this year, it would be different. He would have easily brought her along, but the kids hadn't met her yet. He had told them that he was dating someone because he didn't want Ava to have another reason to turn into

Nancy Drew. That was as far as the conversation had gone, however. He wasn't sure what the protocol was on introducing her. The kids had already known Martin through his daughter, so Melissa hadn't had to navigate any official introductions. Their relationship had grown to the point of group outings with all the kids together. Mack's situation felt quite different. He thought maybe Melissa should meet Aubrey as she should know who their kids were spending time with. Maybe he should talk to Melissa about when she thought was a good time? It seemed there would always be new waters to navigate in this post-divorce life. If only there was a handbook for him.

Back at the office, Antonia greeted him with an update of what he had missed on his long lunch. "The notices are set to go out in the next two days, and there was a call for you from *Law360*. They wanted to talk with you about the Polson Reed case. I took down the number and left it on your desk."

"Really?" Mack asked. "That's great." He called the news service back and set up an interview for just before Thanksgiving. Perhaps this case was going to give a little more than Mack had expected. Publicity for the firm would be fantastic, especially the free kind, and it certainly would put a spotlight on the case.

*

Mack had band practice with Porsche on Thursday night, and he brought the kids along. After the band had finished their practice, the kids asked if they could try a song with the band. Ava and Dev had taken to practicing simple things together at home, and sometimes Mack would join in with his guitar. Jack and Dev worked the drums together, with Dev mostly responsible for keeping a steady beat. Ava played a simple melody over Declan's chords. The kids were aglow after playing with a real band.

"So we have a gig the week after Thanksgiving. It's a company holiday party, seven p.m.," said Jack. "Everyone's good for that Saturday, right?"

Mack ignored the question while everyone else agreed.

"Mack?" Jack prompted.

His kids looked at him.

"You've been practicing with us for months now. Do the gig."

Mack hesitated a moment longer, thinking about the looming final approval, but that hearing wouldn't come until just before Christmas and he had no weekend plans anyway. He could always quit if he needed to, and the practices hadn't been disruptive at all. "Are you sure you want the hairless wonder along?" he asked.

"We want a lead guitarist who knows what he's doing," said Jack.

"Do it, Dad," said Dev. "You can be a rock star instead of a lawyer. I bet it's more fun."

"I'm not quitting law to be in the band, Dev," said Mack. "I'm going to do both."

"Yeah?" Jack asked.

"Yeah," said Mack. "I'm in."

"Great, so over the next two weeks we need to work on reviving the holiday rock songs in our repertoire."

Jack ran through the particulars and then practice was called to an end.

In the car on the way home, Ava asked, "Can we come watch you play?"

"This one is a private event. A lot of them will be, but if a public one comes up, we'll try to work it out with your mom so you guys can come. Keep practicing and maybe you'll get to fill in when Declan or Jack needs a night off."

"Yeah!" Dev yelled from the backseat.

"Your girlfriend could take us to your show sometime too," Ava said.

Mack's brain froze for a beat. "My girlfriend?"

"You said you were dating someone," Ava said. "That's your girlfriend. Or did you break up?"

"No, no, I just…I guess we haven't really used that term yet."

Dev's handheld video game started chiming from the backseat and Mack knew Dev was no longer interested in the front seat conversation.

"You've been going on dates with only her for months now," said Ava. "She's your girlfriend whether you've said it or not."

Who was Mack to disagree with a twelve-year-old girl in the arena of romance? She seemed pretty sure, and she might even be right. Aubrey had invited him home with her for Thanksgiving. That was fairly committed.

"When do we get to meet her?" Ava asked.

"I need to ask your mom first," said Mack. "Maybe after Thanksgiving. We're going to Uncle Neal's place on Thursday morning."

"Awesome!" yelled Dev.

"Is your girlfriend coming?"

"Didn't I just say that you might meet her *after* Thanksgiving? It won't be before, kiddo." Mack would have to have that conversation with Melissa soon or Ava would have it for him.

*

The Wednesday before Thanksgiving, Mack sat down with a reporter from *Law360* in his office. The reporter, Roger, placed a recorder on the table between them. Mack had opted for the more casual space of their breakroom.

"Tell me about this class-action lawsuit you have going on," Roger said. "You're representing the drivers for a rather large company, correct?"

"Yes, Polson Reed Trucking. We've got twelve class representatives and a class size over six hundred. It's been a long road, but we're finally at a settlement of seven million dollars. There's still work to be done, of course, but we're finally seeing action."

"What is the foundation of the lawsuit?" Roger asked.

"Polson Reed hasn't been paying their drivers separately for non-driving time. Rest breaks were totally unaccounted for, and they weren't handling meal breaks appropriately either. We took the rest breaks issue to court and we're suing under PAGA and unfair labor practices. We're calling out the corporate policies in effect that are allowing the company to steal wages from their drivers. Other trucking companies should take notice. If they aren't compensating their drivers equitably, there are ways to call them out and they will be expected to pay the price for taking advantage of their employees."

Roger nodded. "Start at the beginning for me, would you? What was the initial claim and how has that changed?"

Mack answered his questions over the course of the next hour and a half. Then Roger thanked him for his time and told him the article would be running in the January issue, providing the editor approved it.

"Thank you," Mack said. "It's important that when a big company like this messes up, they get called out. They're the ones who can do the most harm because they have the most resources. I appreciate you helping to tell the story of these drivers." He walked Roger out and exhaled. His hairless appearance had made him nervous about the impression he would make on Roger, but the reporter hadn't batted an eye. The article could really be a twist to the screws he had put to Polson Reed and their team of lawyers.

Chapter 24

When Mack picked up the kids for the Thanksgiving weekend, he broached the topic of Ava and Dev meeting Aubrey. The kids were still packing their things for a long weekend at their uncle's house and Mack had arrived a little early just to discuss this. They sat down at the kitchen table with coffees.

"Ava was asking me about meeting Aubrey, and I'd like to know how you feel about the kids meeting her soon," he said.

"Right, well, I guess I'd like to be introduced," Melissa said. "It's not that I think you've developed poor judgment or anything. I just…think that it's only right I be able to recognize her on the street, you know?"

"Makes perfect sense," Mack said. "Maybe the next time I have the kids, you could bring them over to my place and I'll have Aubrey come over?"

"Yeah, okay. Let me know when you have it arranged with her."

"Good. I'm glad that conversation is over, not going to lie," Mack said.

Melissa tapped her coffee mug. "I understand." She cleared her throat. "You're going to Neal's for the weekend?"

"Yes." Mack knew she was already aware of this, but apparently she couldn't think of anything else to say at the moment. "Oh, um, I joined Jack's band."

"After all this time rejecting him? Is he pleased?"

"He seems to be. My first show with them is next weekend. The kids asked if they could come, but it's a private event for a company party. I did say that if I played a public one, I'd try to work it out with you so they could come."

"Of course. That would be great for them to see you doing that. I'm glad you've rediscovered your musical interests. It was—" She stopped abruptly and then seemed to decide to continue. "It was always so endearing when you played lullabies to Ava and then Dev. I have a picture where Ava is sitting in front of you and staring at your hands while you play the guitar. It's one of my favorite pictures of her. She's wide-eyed, entranced."

Mack knew the photo. Melissa meticulously filled photo albums. Even when the camera was digital and they could be stored forever, she made a monthly trip to print the family photos. Then she would spend the evening labeling them with who, when, and where, placing them in albums organized by the years of their lives. The first one began with their honeymoon. He wondered now if that one was in the M&M box in the attic. She was always the best at preserving their memories. What photos would he miss now?

"I was thinking," Mack said, "that photo I sent you of Ava at her voice lesson?"

"Yes?"

"What if we made like a shared photo folder online so that we can share what we capture of the kids? I know we're still going to be present for their big things together, but you were always so good at capturing the small things, like with Ava and me playing guitar. I'd like to still see stuff like that."

"That sounds like a great idea," Melissa said. "Dev said something about doing YouTube videos with you?"

"Oh, yeah, I just mentioned we could play some songs together and put them up on there. He thinks it would be cool. Obviously, I would ask your permission first before he and Ava are on the internet," Mack said hastily when he realized this might be a concern and not just friendly chatting.

"No, I think it's great. It's sort of another way we could share what they're up to. Videos, I mean."

"Well, great. They're really making headway with their instruments of choice. Dev doesn't sound like a bunch of things falling out of a closet anymore."

Dev's rolling suitcase tumbled down the stairs with him thundering behind it. "Sorry, sorry, sorry!" he yelled. "I was trying to put the handle down to carry it and it tipped over and I couldn't stop it!"

"You spoke too soon," Melissa said to Mack. "Nothing's damaged. It was an accident."

"What was that?" Ava appeared at the top of the stairs.

"Suitcase falling down the stairs," Mack said. "It's all good. Are you about ready?"

"Yeah. Two seconds," she said, heading back to her room.

Mack took over Dev's suitcase and brought it out to the car. By the time he had loaded it in, Ava had hers waiting.

*

Upon first arriving, Mack's appearance obviously startled Neal, but it didn't take long for him to grow accustomed to it. Dev spent the weekend on the trampoline with his cousins and Ava plinked away at Neal's piano, trying to match each note with her voice. Neal had played piano since he was seven and the piano was a gift from his in-laws when he and Kristie had married. Ava built a new bond with her uncle when he took over the keys and she sang along. Mack spent some quality time watching football and playing some himself outside with all the kids.

The next week he had his first gig with Porsche. In some ways, he felt twenty-two again, rocking out in front of a crowd, but it was also different. He supposed that was a good thing. Life only went forward and if it felt the same, then he hadn't changed, and change was better than stagnation.

Questions came in from drivers in the class action and Poyfair Law chugged along, answering and resolving everything as quickly as possible. Melissa, Ava, and Dev met Aubrey, and all of them seemed completely fine with it. Mack supposed he had Melissa's dating Martin to thank for making the introduction so easy with the kids.

Melissa left shortly after introductions, and Dev befriended Aubrey immediately. His fondness of facts and her mathematical mind had strong overlap. He told her about playing the drums and then said, "Dad, Ava, and me practice together. We're going to make YouTube videos when Ava and I know more."

"When you know more? I bet you know enough to make one right now," said Mack.

"Do you want to hear us play something? Maybe you can record it?" Dev asked Aubrey.

Aubrey looked at Mack. "Only if your dad wants to, and Ava."

Mack's neck heated. It was one thing to play for an audience, but an audience of one particular person…

"Let's go, Dad." Dev pulled him toward the living room.

The drums had migrated to the communal space now that the three of them were playing music together at times. There was very little room left for company, but Aubrey sat down at the dining table where she could face the living room. She took out her phone and propped her elbows on the table for a steady camera.

"Ready," she said.

They warmed up with "Twinkle, Twinkle, Little Star," and then began "Brown-Eyed Girl," a song Mack used to sing to Ava when she was a baby. Mack forgot to be embarrassed as he started enjoying the collaboration with his kids. He caught Aubrey's smiling eyes and felt even more confident. When they finished the tune, Aubrey stopped her recording and said, "I think that definitely deserves a spot on YouTube."

"I wanna watch it!" Dev scrambled out from behind his drums and around the coffee table to land next to Aubrey. Ava joined them at the table on Aubrey's other side and Aubrey pressed play.

After dinner and some board games, Mack sent the kids to bed and sat with Aubrey for a while.

"I can help you get that video on YouTube, if you want," she suggested, cuddling up against him on the couch.

"Thanks. I guess I really do have to figure out how that works from a creator's side now. It'll be a good activity for us though. It was sometimes difficult to find something both Ava and Dev wanted to do. You saw how they fight over which games to play. Having something we can all enjoy just feels incredibly important now that I'm with them solo. Before the divorce, we could kind of divide up to spend time with them when they wanted to. After, I was looking so hard for something we could do together regularly and then we sort of found it by accident one night when I was playing with the old band and they came along."

"It's not surprising that they both found something you enjoy appealing. They saw you having fun with your friends."

"I guess so."

"Do you think they liked me?" Aubrey asked.

"Absolutely." Mack kissed her on the cheek.*

The *Law360* article came out just after Christmas, and Mack bought a few copies for the office. It was nice timing with the final approval hearing looming that same week. The article presented him rather well and he found himself feeling rather encouraged by it. He had one more meeting with the class representatives to explain the way they structured the settlement.

"The presentation of our settlement is a bit different. We broke it down into tiers and everyone needs to agree to this," Mack said. "The top tier is going to get the most money and it's going to be a little less from there for each tier. You need to agree that you're in the five thousand group or whichever group. You can't be complaining and saying you want to be in the ten group. Here's the deal: Anyone who put their name on the lawsuit, had a deposition taken, testified at trial, and went to the mediation, those are the top tier. It goes down from there into different levels. If anyone starts complaining about the tier they're in, the judge isn't going to go for this settlement. If anyone starts claiming they were at trial when they weren't or were at mediation and they weren't, that's going to shoot us all in the foot. Does everyone understand? Are we all agreed?"

There was a little murmuring, but no one objected.

"Okay. Now, we'd like to make a strong showing of support for the settlement, so I'm asking you all to come to the final approval hearing. This will show the judge that you're on board with the way the settlement is structured. It will help get this thing done."

They all did as he asked. Agreements were signed and every last one of them donned their Sunday best one final time for the lawsuit against their employers. Mack straightened his tie again and again. Gloria tapped a pen on the table in front of him. "Mack, relax. You're making everyone else jumpy."

"Sorry, it's just…the attorney fees, you know? If Judge Keats decides our request for thirty-three percent is unreasonable. He could knock that number down to the basement, you know?"

The figures danced in his head. He was asking for two-point-four million dollars, but Judge Keats would decide if that was reasonable. Mack could walk out of here today with only two hundred thousand coming his way, or even less. That just wouldn't work. He rubbed a hand across his neck and hoped Judge Keats was in an approving mood.

After Keats entered and was seated, he said, "Is Mr. Poyfair not present today?"

"I'm here, Your Honor," Mack said. The last time Keats had seen him, he still had a mostly full head of hair. And he definitely had eyebrows.

Judge Keats didn't linger in his surprise. "Then we will proceed. There's no need for this to take all day and it seems this has been worked out and agreed to. Everything seems reasonable to me, so I'm going to issue the final approval."

Mack's throat clenched. He heard a rustling behind him through the assembled drivers.

"You've been working on this case for nearly two years now and it's been well argued, well researched. Incredibly professional conduct on this. I have to commend you, Mr. Poyfair, on the unusual risks you took in the course of this. The results are impressive. Is there anything you would like to say on the matter before we close this out?"

Mack spoke up. "I want to thank the class representatives for their efforts. It was certainly a burden on them to see this through at times, but they have done their part to get us to this point."

"Do any of the representatives have anything to say?" Judge Keats asked.

Isaiah Garza stood up. "On behalf of all the representatives, I want to say thank you, Your Honor, for being so kind in this. We are grateful to have the matter settled."

The judge closed the session, and everyone exited the courthouse. Mack had cautioned them to reserve any exuberance for outside the building. When they emerged into the cool, overcast January air, there were grins and laughter and tears.

"This is it, yes?" Isaiah asked. "We are done?"

"That was it," Mack confirmed, grinning himself. "Your checks will come in time, but your obligations to attend meetings and hearings are over and the deal is done. You should see a change in how you're paid at work as well."

"Thank you, Mr. Poyfair. Thank you so much for this. This money will be a great help to many of us. It's been a surreal experience."

"After two years," Amanda said, "I'm not sure I can actually believe it is over."

"I promise," Gloria said, "it'll sink in when the check arrives."

Antonia called out, "Will everyone please gather on the steps? I want to get a picture of us all."

The drivers assembled themselves behind Mack and Gloria. Then Antonia stopped a man on his way inside to ask if he would take the photo and she went to stand behind Mack. The man took a few shots and returned Antonia's phone to her. She looked at the photos, pausing on her favorite and said, "That's going on the office wall. I can tell, this is going to be the first of many for us."

Epilogue

Three months later, the checks arrived. Isaiah Garza was awarded eighteen thousand dollars. Others received anywhere between five and fifteen thousand dollars, depending on their involvement in the entire process of the lawsuit. The class members who were not representatives received five thousand dollars each, which was quite the windfall for many of them.

Mack received his entire two-point-four million dollars. For the first time in his life, he wasn't splitting the payday with other partners and that left him in an entirely different position than he was used to. After paying down his line of credit, Mack spoke with some financial advisors who recommended he do some investing. With a little time on his hands after the final settlement of the Polson Reed Trucking case, Mack spent some time researching and learning a little about investments and business. All of it was telling him that the character of a company is determined by its leader. Mack had marked himself as a risk taker from the start of Poyfair Law, and he had seen his risks over the last two years pay enormous dividends. Judge Keats had approved of his risks. So, despite the word from his friends that the investment seemed risky, Mack started researching Tesla. He looked into the owner and saw the same out-of-the-box thinking Mack had applied to his flagship case, and he saw the same risk-taking. He could see the younger generation trending toward electric vehicles and cleaner energy. After buying a new suit and a Hublot watch—something he had dreamed of owning for years—Mack took nearly all of what remained from his fees and purchased stock in Tesla. He was making another bet on his instincts, and the confidence that inspired gave him the capability to run his firm on his mission of thinking big. Poyfair Law began to cater exclusively to workers and consumers taking class action against big businesses.

The End

CPSIA information can be obtained
at www.ICGtesting.com
Printed in the USA
FSHW021453200122
87715FS